MOTHER'S DAY

&

OTHER STORIES

D1518407

JEFF SCHWARTZ

Dedication

*For Deborah, who listened patiently
and encouraged wholeheartedly.*

TABLE OF CONTENTS

Mother's Day Alice's Story 1

Mother's Day Neal's Story 19

Mike's Weekend 35

Mingo Fishtrap 2005 54

Jamal's Story 70

Mom's 80

Epilogue - Next Mother's Day 94

Afterword 100

Acknowledgments 102

MOTHER'S DAY
ALICE'S STORY

Alice Miller was sitting at the outdoor patio of the Lakeside Café that Sunday morning. It wasn't just her usual Sunday morning. It was Mother's Day. As she sipped her coffee and broke a blueberry scone in half, her thought was that this was the first Mother's Day since mom died. Sadly, every Sunday had been difficult since Mom was not there, across the table, reaching out for her half of the scone.

Alice was dressed in navy blue spandex having just come from her Pilates class. This, her Sunday morning ritual: class, then meeting Mom here at the Café afterward. Alice had just turned sixty-four, had never been married and was not in a relationship. Alice felt more alone than she ever remembered.

"Ellen," she called out to the waitress. "I guess I'll take my check now."

Alice is an artist, a painter, and a printmaker. Totally self-supporting her entire career. She did not make a lot of money, but she got by. She made reproductions of her work and was able to sell them on the internet. She was also tied into a Hollywood set designer and her images graced many a wall on both network and cable television shows. After Mom passed away, she had inherited enough money to get by with less concern. Good thing too. She had not produced much new work of late. Creativity and grief were not good partners.

She had come to Columbia, Maryland nearly thirty years ago because Mom was there. Dad had died. Alice came to be with her mom for a while. And stayed. Dad had been a Baltimore cop. Smoked too much, and he ate the clichéd cop diet of burgers and donuts. He had just turned sixty-two when his heart gave out. Mom had been sixty then, and from that time on, she and Mom had been together. They did not live together. Just were usually around each other. Dinner at Mom's apartment once or twice a week. Shopping trips to Baltimore or down to Montgomery County. They traveled. Even took a cruise especially for mothers and daughters. Mom would come by the studio in the afternoon while Alice was painting. Have a coffee, sit and chat. They would go out to dinner at least once a week, maybe more. A lonely older woman and a lonely middle-aged artist. Happy together.

Don't misunderstand. Alice had friends. She was social. She went to parties and art openings. She hung out with couples. Alice told her Mom she dated occasionally. If she was being honest with herself, not that often. Alice fell in love early. It was shortly after college when she was twenty-three. Had her heartbroken after a five-year relationship went sour. She could still hear his words: "I've met someone else. I'm sorry."

She had not met anyone else to get serious with since, even while living in New York for a few years after that. Then Dad passed away, she came back to Columbia and became her mother's companion. Mom died last summer, just weeks short of her 90th birthday. Alice did not regret one day of the time they were together. It was delicious to love and respect someone that much. She had been lost ever since.

Ellen returned with the check and refilled her coffee. "Alice, I've been meaning to ask you how you are doing. I can't get used to your mom not being here. I imagine today, of all days, is a hard one. You should make plans. Stay busy. Your mom will be in your thoughts and in your heart. God Bless."

"Thanks, Ellen. You have that right. I've got the *Mother's Day Blues*. Too bad I can't sing. Hard as it may be for me, I will try to celebrate her life today."

Alice laid a credit card on the check and took out her phone. She thought she might call a friend. See if anybody had anything fun planned for today. That would help. As soon as she pressed the phone icon, her favorites came up. There at the top of her favorites list was the name *"Mom."* She had not had the will to delete the contact. Would anyone?

Alice had convinced her mother to get a cell phone when she turned seventy-five. After all, it was a new century and she was a young seventy-five. She was sharp to the end and the technology never bothered her. And she loved the iPhone commercials. Also, the commercials about falling had the desired effect. Lifeline for Mom was the cell phone which was always close at hand.

It had been over ten months since she died. Alice thought it possible but unlikely that someone new would have her number this soon. Of course, she wouldn't call it. Someone might answer. Then what?

But Alice could not deny a strange urge to communicate. She selected Mom's contact and navigated to the text message icon. They each had gotten in the habit of texting first thing on birthday's, on Christmas and New Year and of course, on Mother's Day. The cell phone had been a revelation for her. She could text Alice random thoughts without feeling she was intruding with a call.

Alice typed, *"Happy Mother's Day, Mom."*

As soon as she hit send, she regretted it. How would she explain this behavior? So pathetic. It certainly could become embarrassing, but hell, a bit of embarrassment never hurt anyone. Something like a wrong number. No big deal. She took the last bite of the scone and finished her coffee. She stood up to leave, threw her backpack over her shoulder, and headed toward the parking garage. The garage was across the street, just down the block. It took good karma on Sunday morning to get parking any closer to the lake.

Alice had not put her phone in the bag. She was carrying it in her hand, almost as if willing a reply from her text. As she walked, she expected the phone to vibrate at any moment. She looked down at it, just for a second, as she was about to step out between two parked cars to cross the street. She looked right, then to the left, there were no cars coming. She had not noticed the bicyclist coming from her right. As she looked left, she stepped out in the street. The bike hit her hard. She went down, her arm and shoulder taking the hit. It must have been both the handlebar and the rather large rider. The cyclist was sprawled across her legs, his bike on top of her. She was in pain nearly to the point of passing out. The phone left her hand and scooted a few feet away.

*****

Officer Joe Kelly had seen it all happen from across the street and fifty yards down the block. He radioed in as he sprinted over. Joe was slightly winded. He took in the scene. He picked up a cell phone from the ground and put it in his pocket while he directed traffic to allow an ambulance to pull in and collect the injured woman when it arrived. The cyclist was dazed but had come down on top of the woman and broken his fall. Kelly helped him up. He seemed startled but uninjured. "Don't leave, please. I'll need to get some information." The cyclist grunted out "I'm fine, thanks for asking." A woman on a bike pulled up, dismounted athletically, and rushed to the man. Kelly turned his attention to the woman on the ground. She was not getting up so quickly. A pedestrian, a young man, had seen the accident and was kneeling next to the older woman who was moaning and in a fetal position. The woman seemed to have a broken arm and maybe a dislocated shoulder. No doubt, she was in shock and pain.

In minutes the ambulance arrived, the Rescue Squad building being less than a mile away. The EMS driver and his assistant secured the women's arm and got her on a stretcher. They started an IV, likely something to calm her down and deal with the pain until they got her to the hospital. Officer Kelly pulled the cell phone from his pocket, certain it was hers, and wanting to make sure it got into the ambulance with the woman. He had her backpack at his feet and reached down inside feeling for a wallet or some other ID.

The EMS guy was in a hurry to get moving. "Does the backpack belong to the injured woman?" he asked. "Better let me have it." He said they would call in her information on the way.

Officer Kelly checked the phone and saw it was open to the message screen. The message that was displayed said "Happy Mother's Day Mom." He called out to the ambulance driver and asked him to wait while he replied to a text. He thought he should alert her family to the situation. He quickly typed, "*Your mother has been in a minor accident and is on the way to County General Hospital. She is OK but has likely broken something. I am sending this phone in the ambulance, so she will have it at the hospital. Officer Joe Kelly. Howard County Police.*"

Joe hit send and stuffed the phone into the backpack. He passed it to the medic in the back of the ambulance. It never occurred to Kelly that the text he sent was not a reply.

Jamal

Jamal was feeling very fortunate today. He had just turned thirty-two and had really gotten his life in order. Hell, not just in order but to a place he had never even dreamed of. He had a beautiful wife, a happy, healthy, baby daughter, and a new job that allowed them to move out of his small apartment in Ellicott City and down to a rented townhouse in Columbia to be near his wife's family. It was Mother's Day and Jamal was set on making Kim's first Mother's Day special. In future years he imagined he'd let little Jeanette do that, but at eleven months it seemed to be asking the impossible for his darling daughter to take that on. It was breakfast in bed. A bit of nursing until the baby fell back to sleep, then get undressed and slip back under the covers to practice the activity that would lead to having more kids.

All Jamal wanted was to have a family and be a good dad. Kim came from a large Vietnamese family who immigrated to Baltimore in the mid-1970s. She had two brothers and a sister. Her parents had nurtured them, but at the same time were very demanding. Kim was smart. They all were. She was a sociologist, who had gotten her first two degrees at the University of Maryland and was working on a Ph.D. at Georgetown. She was only twenty-seven when she started teaching at the community college. He was a twenty-nine-year-old student in the first semester of his second year when he walked into her Introduction to Sociology classroom. Fifty minutes later he walked out in a fog. He was in love.

Jamal had avoided Intro to Sociology his first year. The course description referred to so many things that were painful to him. He knew full well how social conditions and values affected peoples' life chances. Family life was not his past. Jamal was a textbook orphan. He was left under a chair in a basket in a Baltimore hospital waiting room. Likely born in a project apartment or basement to an underaged or drugged-out mother and deposited at the City Hospital for lack of any other options. He never knew. Whenever he asked his foster parents about his name, Jamal Doe, he got an anecdotal version of being named after the actor who played the kid in the Cosby Show and the usual plug-in name for unknowns. What he did know was Social Services, foster homes, and never feeling like he belonged anywhere.

Somehow, he had made it through high school. Thanks to some good teachers and his role as a linebacker on the football team. Coach Perry ran a tight ship and though Jamal was prone to trouble, Coach always reeled him back in. He even attended Jamal's graduation, beaming at him like he had jarred loose the ball from some running back and was racing toward the goal line.

Jamal maintained some communication with a few of his foster parents, but the one he liked best, Ma Thompson, died when he was in middle school. After that, all social services provided him turned out to be a roof over his head and not much parenting. At one point during high school, Jamal figured it all out. The Jaeger's had taken in four foster kids and were collecting significant money from the government. Cash and four teenagers who did most of the house and yard work. A great deal for them. Warm and fuzzy it was not. Mrs. Jaeger, an alcoholic who began with wine after breakfast, was especially cruel. Jamal was light-skinned. She got to calling him half breed. Said he was likely the offspring of a whore who let her customers ride bare-back once too often. Her words stung, but Jamal knew she was an awful person and he had three other fosters in the house to back him up on that.

After high school, at eighteen, with no foster home, no money, and no one encouraging a try at college, Jamal got out of Baltimore and took a job at a McDonald's down in Prince George County. He slept on the couch of a couple of his high school teammates who were going to the University of Maryland and had an apartment in Laurel. That lasted only a month or so until the logistics of not having a car became an issue. Jamal moved back to Baltimore where at least he could get around. More entry-level jobs ensued and within a year, with winter coming, Jamal was thinking of joining the Army and getting away from the life he had wound up with. He enlisted without hesitation. He knew that self-discipline, and the structure the Army provided, much like the football team, was the best way to keep himself from winding up dead or in jail. He had not only watched "The Wire" on television, but Jamal had also watched it on the streets, *up close and personal*, as they say.

To stay off the wrong side of the law he decided to get on the right side. Eight years later he came out of the service having learned to fly a helicopter and then finished up with four years as Military Police. He had been working security at the community college while pursuing a degree in Criminal Justice. Then he found love and family and gained a great deal of perspective about his childhood. He thought back to the moment at the community college, sitting in a philosophy course barely paying attention when the professor projected a quote on the screen.

In the words of CS Lewis: "You can't go back and change the beginning, but you can start where you are and change the ending."

That phrase became the mantra for his life. He realized that he had been doing that. The tours in the Army, a job, and his attempt to get an education were fulfillments of those words. Now, being married to Kim, starting a family, *the ending* had much more promise.

The family had gathered for a Sunday brunch Mother's Day feast. Kim's dad did all the cooking while Kim, her mom, her sister, and two sisters-in-law sat around the living room and played with the children. The mothers were all close in age, the kids, just babies, and toddlers. Jamal and the other dads were in the den with Bloody Marys' made with sake instead of vodka. A family thing he was told.

The family knew that Jamal was unhappy on holidays such as Mother's Day and Father's Day. Not that he was that sensitive to it anymore. It was an old wound that would never quite heal. Jamal had found a family and they had accepted him completely. They were immigrants who came to the United States right after the Vietnam War. They were very experienced in the subject of acceptance. As he watched his wife's family enjoy each other, it still made him a little sad that he had no mother or father to call or spend any time with on these holidays.

The family dining table was round and sat ten, just like being in a restaurant. The kids had settled down. The infants sat on their mom's laps while the older ones ate at a small play table their grandparents kept in the house for crafts and containment. The two and three-year-olds never complained about not being at the grown-up table. They loved their special place which their grandmother set with a tablecloth and a battery-powered candle in the middle.

Jamal had just finished a small bowl of black pepper chicken and rice. It was his favorite Vietnamese dish. His phone vibrated in his shirt pocket, indicating a text message. He took it out and saw the message. It read "Happy Mother's Day Mom." One thing was certain, *he* was nobody's "Mom." His phone was new last month. He chuckled to himself at the irony. He ignored the text in favor of a second helping of rice and the various meats and broth set out in bowls for a family meal.

His father-in-law looked up at him questioningly, he asked, "Is that a text you need to deal with?" Jamal shook his head and waved off the query with a slight wave of his hand.

It was barely ten minutes later that his phone vibrated again.

Jamal was unsure of what to do. He told the family what the first text said. Kim spoke up quickly to clarify "Jamal has a new phone and a new number. Remember he shared his new number with all of you when he got it."

Jamal cut her off by passing her the phone. "Read the second text, he said."

Kim read aloud, "*Your mother has been in a minor accident and is on the way to County General Hospital. She is OK but has likely broken something. I am sending this phone in the ambulance, so she will have it at the hospital. Officer Joe Kelly. Howard County Police.*"

When Kim passed the phone back to Jamal, he said. "I'll call back and explain that I'm not her son." The call went directly to voicemail. He disconnected.

The family did not give him much choice. His mother-in-law spoke up.

"Jamal, there's a woman in the hospital; you don't know who she is, but you do know she is hurt. You should go check it out. You are studying to be a detective, go detect. You may be the only one who knows where she is."

"Really Mrs. Li, I'm not sure I can be of any help. Me, today, Mother's Day, looking for a woman who sent a text to her kid and then was in an accident? Find her and do what? They'll sort it out at the hospital."

His father-in-law shook his head, seemingly displeased with Jamal's reaction, and began to rise from his chair. "I'll go. It won't take long and someone needs to go. The way this is happening it would seem to be our responsibility." Kim's dad believed in such things as karma and destiny.

Jamal froze a bit at Kim's dads' response but quickly stood. "No, I'll go. You are right, Mrs. Li, sit down Mr. Li, I should go. This is on me and I can't allow my ancient history to color my judgment. I was being an ass."

*****

Jamal made the ten-minute drive over to County Hospital to find who knows who and hope he might be of help. He pulled into visitor parking and assumed he should go to the emergency room where someone in an ambulance would be taken. He waited behind a woman at the check-in desk who was asking about her son. He had apparently severed his thumb while slicing a loaf of crusty bread. She was frantic. "Would they be able to sew it back on?" she asked. The nurse replied "We expect so ma'am. You need to calm down. Why don't you go sit down and I will get you when we know more? "

A bit intimidated, it was Jamal's turn to explain what he needed. He said to the nurse, "Excuse me. Was a woman recently brought in by ambulance? An accident victim?"

The nurse looked up at him questioningly. "Do you have a name?"

Nervously, Jamal replied; "Yes my name is Jamal."

The nurse looked at him strangely.

"No sir, the name of the injured party. The name of the woman who was brought here by ambulance."

Jamal felt foolish. He almost wished he had not come. He had no idea what he would do if the found the person. He tried to explain.

"Ma'am, I received a text from a police officer who seemed to believe that he was sending the text to the child of this woman because it had followed a text that said *Happy Mother's Day Mom.*"

The nurse, at first, seemed confused. She had a funny look on her face. Then suddenly Jamal thought he saw a light go on as if it had all become crystal clear.

She smiled and asked; "So the person who was brought in was your mother?"

Apparently understanding him was not in the cards.

"No," Jamal replied. "The police officer who sent the text thought she was my mother. I assumed that since the police officer was texting my number, then it was probable that no one else has been notified that the woman is here. My family insisted that I come and see if I could be of any help."

"Well Jamal, this is highly irregular. You've come to check on a woman and you have no idea who she is."

Jamal smiled. "Yes ma'am, I guess that's true. Look at my phone. Read the texts yourself. What would you think?"

The nurse, whose name tag read "Jackie," looked at the phone then thought a moment. "Let's take a walk down the hall, you dial the number from the text on your phone and if we hear it ring it will bear out your story." And ring it did. In Exam Room 3. Jackie stopped and smiled.

"Okay, Jamal. Yes. A woman just was brought in with a bruised shoulder and a broken arm, but she will be fine. Her arm is in a cast and she is a little groggy from the pain meds. Let me take you in and introduce you. Her name is Alice Miller."

Jackie knocked softly. There was no reply. She quietly opened the door. There on the bed, one arm in a sling, big scrape across the cross her cheek all the way up to her forehead, dozed an older woman.

'She may be a bit out of it," Jackie said, "Why don't you sit in the chair and give her a few minutes? Then you can try to speak to her." With that, Jackie turned and left the room.

Alice

Alice sensed someone else in the room. She opened her eyes and saw a large, young African American man sitting in the chair next to her bed. She did not recognize him. She assumed he might be hospital staff just watching over her. She looked over at him and smiled.

"I'm feeling a bit better if that's why you're here. To check on me?" She continued, "I don't know how I could've been so clumsy; I don't remember anything after I stepped out into the street to cross over to my car, and suddenly, I was on the ground with a bicycle lying across me and a man in Lycra and a helmet sprawled alongside me. Are you a doctor?" she asked. The young man just stared at her. He seemed at a loss for words.

After a pause, he said, "No, Mrs. Miller, my name is Jamal Doe. I received a text. Two really. The first one said, "Happy Mother's Day, Mom," and the second one came from a police officer named Kelly. It basically said: 'Your mom's been in an accident and has been taken to County Hospital.' Since I never knew my mother, I knew that wasn't possible. I was at brunch at my in-laws and the whole family insisted that I come over and see what it was about."

A tear ran down Alice's cheek. "Actually, it's Miss Miller. I am not married and have no children." She was so embarrassed and suddenly sad. Now she would have to explain to this young man how she had gotten him involved in her day.

"Jamal, I know you could not have sent me that text because I wrote it. I wrote it to my mom who obviously had that phone number before you. I never imagined they gave out numbers so quickly. The policeman must not have noticed the text was outgoing."

Alice and Jamal wound up talking for over an hour. She shared her story of Mother's Day morning and apologized for allowing her grief to spill over on him. They connected about her growing up a policeman's daughter and the fear she and her Mom lived with when he was on duty. Jamal told her of his time as an MP in the Army and how he had studied Criminal Justice at the community college while working as a security officer. He told her a few stories about things that happened on campus during his watch.

He wondered out loud, "Did you and your mom ever get used to the fear and anxiety of your dad being at risk as a policeman? My wife Kim says for me not to think about it."

Alice laughed. "I can tell you from experience that she probably means she will think about it enough for both of you."

The more she told him of her life as an artist and being single and not just caring for her mom, but having her as a friend, the more he opened about his own past without parents. When he got to the part about returning home from the Army and going back to school, he blushed with embarrassment.

"I fell in love with my Sociology professor and married her. Am I a cliché or what? Sometimes I feel like a character in a totally transparent romantic comedy. Sappy ending and all. The orphan who ends up in a real family with a child of his own. My own version of '*Annie*.'"

His reflections led Alice to say something she had never said aloud and barely acknowledged as true. "Jamal, I have had a pretty good life. I love making art and I have no regrets at all about spending the better part of thirty years as my mom's best friend and companion. But now I'm alone." A tear slowly ran down her cheek. "You, on the other hand, are here because despite the life you were born to, you are a caring soul whose family has encouraged you to become yet a better man. You have Kim, Jeanette, and an extended family to ensure you will not be alone in the future."

Alice closed her eyes and turned her head away. Jamal said nothing in reply to her words. The silence lasted a minute or so, then his phone buzzed a text coming in. It was Kim. The text simply said, "So?"

Jamal stood, excused himself and left the room. A few minutes later he returned and sat down. He smiled when he looked at Alice. "It's all been taken care of."

"What has?" Alice asked.

Jamal explained, "Kim will get a ride to the hospital when they are ready to release you. She will drive my car home, dropping us off at your car on the way. I will drive you home later. The nurse, her name is Jackie, agreed to release you if I would stay with you for the next four to six hours before leaving you alone."

Alice objected, saying, "Please stop making such a fuss over me. I didn't share my grief with you in exchange for pity. I can call a friend."

Jamal cut her off. "This is not making a fuss, and surly not pity." Listen to yourself. You may not be anyone's mom, but you define being a friend. Let me follow that example. Please come to my in-law's house for dinner. Everyone wants to meet you, and I want you to meet my family. I'll get you home once you feel better. No arguments!"

*****

In the weeks and months that followed, it became a tradition for Alice to join the Li's on Sunday afternoons, for their weekly dinner together. On most Sunday mornings Jamal showed up at the café by the lake, Jeanette in tow. It started out that he would split the scone with Alice as her mom used to do. Then, one Sunday, when Ellen, her regular waitress came by with a tray already filled with two coffees, a glass of milk, and a blueberry scone,

Alice looked up at her and smiled. "Ellen, we are going to need two of those scones from now on." Jeanette seemed to be getting more than a small share and was growing up quickly. Soon they'd need to order three. Alice sat back and watched Jamal be a daddy. He and

Jeanette held hands as they nibbled their share of the scone. She laughed when Jamal poured milk into her sippy cup and pretended to drink it instead of his coffee. Alice knew he was a great dad. She had learned that a Vietnamese family is, indeed, very welcoming. Jamal and Kim were becoming the children she never had. Jeanette was like a grandchild to her. The outcome was too storybook to be true. The only grief she allowed herself now was that her mom would never know them and see the serendipity of it all.

Jamal

For Jamal, it was as though he finally had a mother. So much so that early the next year Jamal went to court and changed his and Jeanette's last name to "Miller" from Doe, which he had always hated. It was a constant reminder that he knew nothing of his true name or where he came from.

Kim had retained her family name, "*Li*." That was how she was known at the college. That evening, however, Jamal had caught her sitting on the couch with a legal pad signing "*Kim Miller*" down the page as if she was considering how it suited her.

When Jamal awakened on the Sunday morning of Mother's Day the following May he quietly slipped out of bed, grabbed his phone off the nightstand and headed for the kitchen to make Kim her Mother's Day breakfast in bed. Before he even started the coffee, he picked up his phone and grinned like an idiot as he wrote a text message to Alice.

"Happy Mother's Day Mom."

MOTHER'S DAY
NEAL'S STORY

I woke up and it was Sunday morning. Not just any Sunday morning. It was Mother's Day. I haven't liked Mother's Day much since mom died. It has been over a year, March 18th of last year to be precise. I didn't finish that first Mother's Day very well. I think I got drunk. Not think, know. Bourbon and beer. Right after a Sunday morning Bloody Mary. Made sure to blank out the whole day. That was last year. It was all very raw back then. I had not been a very good son.

I can't believe I hadn't spoken to her for nearly six months before she died. We argued. A lot. She disagreed with every decision I ever made. Not that I always made great decisions. "Live and learn." My motto. I finally told her to "stay the fuck out of my life." She did. Then she had a heart attack, alone in the shower. The cell phone I made her get, out of reach, likely stuck in a coat pocket. Out of reach, if she even recalled where she put it.

I remember the day I brought it to her. "Mom, I said." "You should learn to use this phone and keep it close. You live alone and no one would know if you needed help. Press the button on the right side to turn it on." She fumbled with the phone a bit. Finally, she got the screen with the keypad to "*dial*" a call. She put it to her ear, looked at me like I was dumb as a stone and said, "Neal, what kind of junk is this? It doesn't even have a dial tone!" I was too frustrated with her to see the humor. In hindsight, it was me. I was over thirty and she was still mothering and hovering. I just snapped at her once too often and we were done.

Without anyone to help her, she died right there on the bathroom floor. My only salvation was not being the one who found her. Her next-door neighbors, the Harrisons, had gotten concerned since the newspaper was still on the front walk and her car had not moved all day. Jim Harrison told me that he knocked and rang the bell for several minutes before using the key Mom had given him for emergencies. He told me, "It had been eerily quiet when I entered and knew I'd not like what I'd find."

I spent the first three months after she died cleaning out the house in Fair Lawn. The house where I had grown up. I was going to sell it. Then I found I could not even call a realtor to talk about listing it. I gave up my apartment in Teaneck and moved back to the house. I had convinced myself I would rent out a room or two, but that never happened either. Being there by myself, I could almost feel her presence. I was living in my old room because even after a fresh coat of paint the master bedroom still smelled like Mom. Likely more imaginary than real.

Do I sound like we had unfinished business? You bet. Who wants the last thing you ever say to your mom to be "fuck off"? Mother's Day. Here it was again. This made-up Hallmark holiday, making sure I remembered.

She had one birthday for me to get past since she died, October 20th. Not an easy day for me either but at least the whole country wasn't celebrating their mothers that day. Facebook alone would crush my spirits today. Lots of sweet mommy praise and many RIP posts. I decided I needed a diversion. Best way to start a diversion—Bloody Mary, some weed, and some food.

I made up the Bloody at home. Smoked a bowl. Grabbed a jacket and went off to the greasy spoon diner around the corner on River Road. It was cool for May but not unusual. I remember going to baseball games with my dad in the spring, wearing winter coats, and looking for hot chocolate to keep warm.

Dad did not deal well with Mom either. He walked out the day I graduated from high school. He told me he had held out for as long as he could and now, we were both on our own. Dad was in his late thirties when I was born. Thirty-eight, if my math is right. Before Mom, he had been married to his high school sweetheart, but that only lasted four years. Afterward, he focused on his law practice and was made a partner before he was thirty. Mom was a para-legal at his office. Beautiful. Dark hair, dark eyes, still in her twenties. She bedazzled him and they married soon after. I wish I would have known her then. She told me that they were never sure if they wanted children but felt blessed when I came along a few years later. I think they were happy for a time, but Mom's anxiety and manias became more and more difficult to deal with. By the time I have any clear memory of her, at four or five I imagine, she was a bit of a shrew, yelled a lot, mostly at Dad. I understood why he left but I felt abandoned, nonetheless. He was gone and completely absent from my life. I was conflicted about what role I was now meant to play. My confusion may have led to Mom being so protective and hovering over my every move. Dad went to the west coast. Opened a law practice in Santa Monica. Nearly 14 years ago. We talk from time to time. I went out there once or twice after college. He did come back for the funeral. He even handled some of the arrangements and handled the estate. He is a lawyer, after all. That stuff he could handle. Mom's depression and moods, not so much. He had been pretty good to us in his absence. He made a good living practicing law in California. Remarried but never had any more kids. He was over seventy years old now, the retirement age for many, but he claimed that California had kept him young and he had no intention of retiring any time soon. Mom had continued to work as a paralegal at the firm in New Jersey where they had met, but only for a short time. It was awkward, being the ex-wife of a former part-ner. She was left with a 401K. She also got herself a good chunk in the divorce. She didn't die broke. Just alone.

Dad paid my way through college at Rutgers. I fol-lowed his track and applied to Seton Hall Law School, his alma mater. I quickly became a disappointment to both him and Mom when I dropped out after one semes-ter. I hated law school. I was uninspired and not doing well. Sure, I may have partied too much but at the end of the day, I just did not want to be there. I was a bass player in a band for a while, which is what I loved doing, but could not make ends meet and gave it up. I've worked at one thing or another since. Waiter, bartender, and now I've worked my way up to Assistant Manager at a chain restaurant. I didn't need him or her. I was a survivor. I was happy. Until she died without a word from me in all those months.

When I pulled open the door to the diner the smell of bacon and coffee overtook those thoughts of Mom. I was slightly buzzed from the weed and hunger pangs began at first intake of breath. The place was packed. I had a choice of the counter or, if I held back a minute, a two-top booth near the kitchen door was just vacated. I opted to wait. The counter created the possibility that the seat on either side could be occupied by some chatty asshole. That would certainly not fit my mood.

I slid into the booth as soon as the busboy had it cleared and taken a swipe with his rag. A cliché of a waitress flipped a menu in front of me. Out of the corner of her mouth as she walked by, I heard, "Coffee?" and I caught her backward glance with a nod of my own. Pink and white uniform, pencil behind her ear, hair in a bun, cute as a button, and a name tag reading "Gracie." I remembered her from late-night visits after work.

Good god, I love Jersey diners. Back when we were still talking, I would meet Mom for dinner. It would always be at one diner or another. She liked diners because the menu covered it all, Greek, Italian, seafood, steaks, you name it. This way she did not need to decide what cuisine she wanted in advance. She found decisions difficult. She could not even commit to an Italian dinner at an actual Italian restaurant. Memories. So much for a trip to a diner helping me deal with Mother's Day.

Gracie returned with my coffee. Pad in hand she grunted; "What'll it be cutie pie? I haven't seen you in here in a while."

"I've been in. Haven't seen you either, Gracie. I work at a restaurant now and I get most of my meals there. Some nights when it's too busy to take a break I'd wind up hungry on my way home and stop in. You worked nights then."

She cocked her hip a bit, gave me a pure fifties diner look. "Yeah, now I'm in at six a.m. and out at two. You should come back around then, take a walk with me." She winked then paused several seconds, opened her pad, then said: "What can I get you?" As if the rest never happened. Flirting for tips I assumed.

I muttered, "Pancakes Supreme Breakfast." Two eggs over easy, bacon, sausage, ham and a stack of griddle cakes. I was very hungry. I laid my cell phone on the table and nestled into the corner of the booth, sipping the hot coffee and staring at the phone. I opened my favorites intending to pick out someone who might want to hang out today. I must have a friend who is not visiting his mother today. Someone whose mom doesn't live around here. As I scrolled down, I paused. There she was. How could I delete the contact on my phone that said, "Mom"? Nearly pressing the name to dial I recalled her birthday; October 20th, crying and typing a text: "Happy Birthday Mom." And then I remember pressing send. I waited. My cheeks running with tears like I was willing the phone to connect to the dead. What an app that would be. Yet there was nothing. All I wanted was to kid with her about the "important" people who were born on her birthday. Growing up I'd hear, "You know; Mickey Mantle was born on my birthday." When I got old enough to play it back, I would answer, "and Tom Petty" and later on would I tease her with, "and Snoop Dogg." She'd just laugh and say, "They

24

ain't the Mick." If you grew up in North Jersey in the late 1950s and 60s, you were a Yankee fan and Mickey Mantle was it. You could still say that today and not get an argument, regardless of how you felt about Willie Mays and Duke Snider. Dad had made sure both Mom and I understood that.

I sat and stared at her contact on my phone until the waitress plopped two plates down in front of me. One with eggs and meats and another with a stack of three pancakes. Did I just order all that?

Before I picked up my fork, I pressed the message button and opened to my "favorites" and pressed for a new message screen to "Mom." I quickly typed *"Happy Mother's Day, Mom,"* hit the send arrow, grabbed the salt and pepper and went to work on my breakfast feast.

Liz

Liz's cell phone chirped in her hand. A text. It said; *"Happy Mother's Day Mom."* She spoke aloud; "I guess somebody has not updated their contacts in a while, but their mother, really?" Liz had gotten this phone number when she arrived in North Jersey last September. She remembered it clearly because the Verizon store was just across the street from the Residence Inn she lived in before moving into her apartment on October first. New job. In the city where she always wanted to be, New York. She had not bothered with a landline and got a new cell phone when she moved to Fort Lee in order to have a local number rather than a Texas exchange. She wanted the people she met in New York, both socially and at work, not to think of her like a cowgirl from Texas.

Liz had come from Dallas. At thirty-nine, she had finally gotten her dream job at the New York Times. She had worked the Metro Desk at the Dallas Morning News. A colleague who had moved to New York a few years ago had recommended her and lo and behold she got the Times job. Liz was attractive, still a slender 5'8" and now her previously long blonde hair had been cut fashionably short, going for the journalist look rather than glamour. She had accepted the fact that she had been covering the grayish-white strands for over five years, but she was starting to get a bit touchy about turning forty.

Liz had gotten married in her early twenties, right after college, but that only lasted two years and she had been single ever since. She started out in Austin after graduation from the University of Texas and mistakenly had married her college boyfriend. It turned out to be a cliché. He was not ready to be married. He still wanted to hang out with his frat brothers. He even spent several nights a week on campus at the fraternity house, watching sports and getting drunk. After the divorce, she moved on to Dallas for a better job. At this point in her life, over a dozen years later, she reflected that she had sacrificed a lot for her career. Liz admitted to herself that even though she had gotten exactly what she wished for she was feeling a bit lonely and displaced in Northern New Jersey.

The text came from another New Jersey number. She recalled last October, around a month after getting the new phone, a similar text had come in saying; "Happy Birthday Mom." She had thought nothing of it, knowing she had just gotten the phone and figuring someone had simply forgotten to delete this number.

Now someone was texting again, thinking that this was still their mom's telephone. Odd, after so long, but not impossible. Maybe their mom had several numbers and they just didn't delete this one.

She wrote back *"You should update your contacts. How can you not know your mother's number? And you send a text on Mother's Day? Really? I got this phone over six months ago and I am not anyone's mom. This is not her number anymore. Thanks."*

Whoa, that was a little harsh. And on Mother's Day morning. Why did she say all that? She should've just sent *"You have the wrong number, sorry."* Was turning forty making her a little crazy? She didn't imagine she would ever be a mom. Over forty and pregnant? Don't think I'm cut out for that, she thought. She had no man in her life anyway. And no prospects. Maybe, she should write back again and apologize? Before she could even start typing a new message, her phone chirped again.

This time it said; *"Sorry about that. My name is Neal. It was my mom's number. She died."*

Liz was speechless. Harsh? How about cruel and in-sensitive. She had never thought of that. Someone grieving and texting messages to his dead mother. Crazy? Maybe. But who knows? If her Mom had recently died, she could almost see herself doing it. It just had never occurred to her. She had already called her mom this Mother's Day morning. Right at ten o'clock eastern time, eight a.m. back in Denton, Texas. Liz knew that her mom would be sitting with her first cup of coffee and reading the Dallas newspaper. She kept telling Liz how much she missed seeing her daughter's byline. Liz had postponed a Mother's Day visit, in favor of a birthday visit coming up in June that could be bundled with Father's Day. She could get her mother an online subscription to the New York Times and teach her how to use it. Besides, her older brother Mark, his wife Helen, and their two kids were driving up from Austin to spend Mother's Day with the grandparents. Mark had a long history of getting his little sister off the hook.

She stared at the text reply, feeling bad about it, and wrote back once more; *"Neal, my name is Liz. If I were your mom, I'd be happy to know you were thinking of me today and would hope you were happy and getting on with your life."*

Neal

I had just taken the last bite of my eggs when the phone vibrated again. Another text had come back from Mom's number. The previous reply seemed annoyed and rather snarky, stating that they weren't anyone's mom and making clear that they were certainly not mine. Maybe I should have said more than simply, *"She died,"* he thought. I should have explained why I had such a bad case of the Mother's Day blues. How I could not stop feeling so guilty about how it ended with Mom? Broken up because I couldn't go back and apologize for the way I behaved? I was thinking about how hard she had tried to help me find my way. I couldn't blame Mom for the way she was. Of course, she couldn't help me; she couldn't help herself. Now that she is gone, I realize that rather than rejecting her annoying ways of trying to help me, I should have been the one to help her. I should have noticed when she stopped taking care of herself. And of course, she refused to quit smoking cigarettes. Then, after she died, I found antidepressants in her medicine cabinet. She didn't seem to eat right either; lots of carbs. Mostly things I did not know about her until I cleaned out the house. Probably because I shut her out.

When I opened the text and read what "Liz" had written, I began to tear up. I needed to get out of this place before I was openly weeping in public. I threw a twenty down, caught the waitress eye and pointed to it. I was out the door before she reached the table.

Liz

Liz had rented an apartment along the Hudson River facing New York City. She could not afford what she wanted in midtown, so she compromised for a larger place and the view across the river. She liked the place because she could curl up on her couch and look out at the lights of the city. She also liked it because she could have free parking for her car and would be able to drive off into the country in just a matter of minutes. She loved the drive up the Palisades Parkway toward Rockland County. After long weeks at the paper, usually working odd hours, the drive along the cliffs of the Hudson calmed her and helped her not miss Texas as much.

Liz had gone on with her day and by noon she was doing her first load of laundry. She was also able to get more amenities in New Jersey, starting with an in-unit washer and dryer. It always gave her the creeps to be in some basement laundry room. In the movies, the pretty girl usually met the man of her dreams bent over a washing machine with a fistful of quarters. In real life not so much. She had just transferred her whites to the dryer and started a dark load in the washer when her phone rang. It showed up as that number again. The one she had texted back to. Why would this guy Neal be calling her? She hesitated but answered anyway. "Hello, this is Liz. Is this Neal?"

"Liz," he said. "I am so embarrassed. A grown man should not be dragging a stranger into his miserable Mother's Day. I don't usually act this way. To answer your question, when it comes to my Mom, no I am not getting on with my life and I am not very happy. If you were my mother, I hope I would treat you better than I treated my own. I really blew it with her."

Liz could hear the pain and sadness in his voice. She asked if he had any brothers or sisters. "No" he replied.

She then said, "I have an older brother in Austin. He's a musician. Can't toss a pebble in Austin without hitting a musician in the eye. I know we would be there for each other if anything bad happened. It would likely be a lot easier to get through losing your mom if you had a brother or sister to share the grief with. If you are indeed a grown man, then I don't imagine I'm old enough to be your mother. You could talk to me like a sister though."

Neal

She asked me about myself. She seemed curious and had begun by asking lots of questions. I didn't know where to start. I really did not want to do this on the phone, so, after a few minutes, I posed an alternative.

"Liz, are you seeing your mother today?"
She replied, "No, she lives in Texas."

"I live in Fair Lawn. You?"

"Fort Lee."

"I have an idea. I am really feeling alone today. Would you please consider having dinner with me? You seem to be trying to get me to talk about my mom anyway. You could, as you said, be like the sister I don't have. We could meet in the middle. Say, six o'clock at the Houston's off Route 4 in Hackensack?"

"Well, I don't know," hesitant but sounding like she was considering it.

"I get it, I said. I'm the crazy guy who sends texts to his dead mom. But truthfully, it is always busy there, easy drive in and out. A very safe place for dinner with a stranger. I'll wait out front. Dark hair, black blazer, and jeans. If you see me and don't feel comfortable just walk away. I would understand."

It was quiet for a few seconds. "Okay, I guess so. But make it seven."

I arrived a few minutes early and was standing out front when a tall slender woman with short blonde hair emerged from the parking lot. It had begun to rain lightly. Just a mist. She seemed unperturbed about getting wet. She hesitated and scanned toward the front door. She appeared to relax when she saw me. Liz looked younger than she sounded on the phone. I wonder if she'll think this is like a date or something. I may be an emotional mess, but women still seem to see me as; "*tall, dark, and handsome.*" At least, according to the staff at work. They like to tease. Always pointing out which customer looked at me like I was on the menu. Male or female. Maybe they weren't sure about me since I never hit on anyone, customer or employee. I give Liz an easy smile and a wave.

"You must be Liz," I said. "I'm Neal, Neal Amato."

"Elizabeth Tanner, Liz is good" she replied.

I opened the door and she walked in ahead of me. As we approached tonight's hostess, Sybil, she looked up surprised. "Neal, she said, I thought you were off today."

Liz turned to me, a puzzled look on her face. "You work here?"

"Yes, Assistant Manager. Sorry I didn't mention that. I just thought it would be good to come to someplace easy to find, where I knew we could get a table on Mother's Day. I do have to admit I also wanted to show you that I'm not a total screwball. Don't you feel safer already?"

Liz didn't say anything at first. I must have caught her off guard. She gave me an odd look and said, "Any more surprises?"

"No. Just dinner and some conversation. I really appreciate your agreeing to meet me after I made such a fool of myself. I didn't want to be alone tonight."

As we walked to the table Liz leaned in and asked, "How old are you anyway?"

l puffed out proudly, "I will be thirty-two in July, and you, are certainly too young to be my mother."

We were quickly seated in a cozy booth along the back wall of the bar area, water and menus in place. Liz appeared flattered by my remark and couldn't hide the smirk that was rapidly becoming a smile.

"I am turning forty soon," she admitted. "You are nearly a decade younger. You literally represent another generation. A very good looking representative, however."

As I turned beet red, I began asking questions, rapid-fire. "So, you're from Texas? Why are you in New Jersey? What do you do?"

She laughed. "Slow down young fella. I'll tell all," she fired back. "I'm from Denton, Texas, went to UT in Austin, graduated in Journalism, had a starting job there, then Dallas Morning News, now the pinnacle, The New York Times. I work mainly on the Metro Desk, do some investigative, some human interest. I would need to know you a bit longer to give up any other juicy details."

"What about your brother, the musician. Is he in a band I would know?"

"No. He had friends who went on the road and became known, but he stayed local. Has a wife and kids. He invented a phone APP with a friend early on in iPhone history, sold out his share so he could have a nest egg and play music whenever he wanted."

I began to talk about the details of losing my mom. When I finished the story, including the embarrassment of living in my old room in the house, I was tearing up. "I just don't know how to get past this voice in my head that keeps repeating the last words I said to her. I was a happy guy before. I'm a good musician, I've written some music. I've advanced quickly here at Houston's. I can do whatever I set my mind to. I'll be fine. It's just the *Mother's Day Blues*. I should write a song."

Liz had been quiet. Reporters are good listeners. "Make sure you put in a part about not hurting the ones you love." She said.

I took a deep breath and collected myself a bit. I began forming that grin again. I really liked this woman. She made me feel I could be myself. "You hungry? I told our waitress to wait for my signal before coming over." The grin became a smile.

Liz smiled back, looked into his big brown eyes, and under her breath she muttered; "I may not want to be like a sister either."

MIKE'S WEEKEND

Mike Bloom was one of the good guys. A good father, a good husband, a good employee, an all-around nice guy. The coming weekend was going to be special. Mike had to make it special. Not only is Sunday Mother's Day, but Saturday is his wife Maggie's forty-first birthday. Making it special is the minimum. After the mess he made of her fortieth, he must add a major "Wow Factor."

The kids are doing their part. Jake is eleven and Annie is nine. Old enough to help execute the plan, but the plan needed to be his. Making it special was up to Mike. Up to him, to a point. Actually, up to him to do whatever Maggie wanted. His plan would kick off on Friday afternoon when he would pick up the kids at school so Maggie wouldn't have to do it. He would then take them all out for a special evening. Birthday eve you might call it. Living in Columbia, Maryland gave him choices. Baltimore is a short drive north, and Washington, D.C., not too much further to the south. He had considered two Friday night food choices. They could go for crab cakes at G & M, over by the airport or go to downtown Baltimore and do a Little Italy neighborhood restaurant like Sabatino's. He chose Baltimore for Friday and to leave the crab cakes for a Saturday lunch in D.C. What he had up his sleeve for Friday night after dinner and for Saturday's day trip to Washington would provide the "Wow Factor." Saturday night would be a *stay at home* night. No party. Just him and Maggie. Alone. Wow again. Mother's Day would be Maggie's choice.

For the adventure in D.C. Mike called Josh Hiller, an old college friend, who works for the National Park Service. He mentioned to Mike, recently, that he was working on the forgotten 43,000 sq. ft. basement under the Lincoln Memorial called *The Undercroft*.

He had called Josh's cell number. "Hey buddy, how have you been? Still working on that project at the Lincoln Memorial?" "Sure am," Josh said. "And it still freaks me out like it did when I was a kid and my folks took me on a candlelight tour. Still eerie, damp and cold." Mike knew the story. It was how Josh wound up at the National Park Service. His parents had taken him on a tour of the Lincoln Memorial Undercroft. They'd found asbestos down there in the late 1980s and stopped the tours completely. But now the National Park Service was going to re-open the site and create viewing areas and the like. Lucky for Mike, it was Josh on the renovation team. He was trusted with keys. "How possible would it be to take us in for a peek on Saturday? It's Maggie's birthday and she doesn't want a party. I'm thinking she and the kids have no idea the Undercroft exists. Maggie grew up in Ohio and I'm certain our kids don't have a clue."

After the Undercroft and lunch, the next stop would be courtesy of the production manager at a music club down by the lake here in Columbia. Mike had been having a beer at the bar after a show last week. A musician friend, also from his college days, had moved to Austin and had given him a heads up about this hot soul-pop band, *Mingo Fishtrap*. He had opted to come to the show alone. Maggie had blown off going out on a school night. She had said, "I know you love having this new club nearby where national acts stop on tour. Go ahead and have a night out. You need a break." She had told him long ago that their marriage would work best if they could do whatever they felt worth doing. They tried hard not to fight or, at least, ever go to bed angry.

Mike was at the bar having a beer. The show had just ended, and people were quickly exiting the room. Mike was in no hurry. He was going to max out his "break" and chill a bit. The guy who had been in the booth running sound and lights sat down on the stool beside him with a beer of his own. He was relaxed now that the show was over. The band had blown away the room. He nodded and held up his beer in toast fashion, then asked the usual questions. "Did you like the show? Have you seen them before? I'm Harris – I produce the shows here."

"I'm Michael, but everyone calls me Mike. Yeah, I saw you at the board. Great job. The band sounded amazing. The singer, the horns, the groove. I loved it."

Harris was soft-spoken, mid-thirties, and seemed in no rush to leave. He said, "My job mainly is working a larger club in DC, but I get to come out to Columbia on occasion. I really like it out here and I chill at the club after shows whenever I can."

"Oh, you're from D.C.?" Mike asked. "I'm taking my wife and kids down there next Saturday. It's her birthday and I'm trying to do some unusual things." He told him of the morning plan. "Do you happen to have any other ideas that I could wow my wife with on a Saturday in May?"

Harris replied, "I know about the Undercroft. When I was a kid, living in Bethesda, my parents went there. I always felt cheated when my parents did cool stuff like that and didn't take me along." Then he grinned and said, "Have you ever been to the Mansion on O St?" He went on, "The Mansion is a boutique hotel and a museum. Thousands of collectibles have been donated and are all for sale in support of the endeavor. And are there ever collectibles. You need to see it."

They formed a plan. Mike invited him to meet up at the Memorial and the quid pro quo was that Harris had complete access to the Mansion and would give them a top to bottom tour they would never forget.

*****

When Thursday afternoon finally came, Mike thought he had a pretty good plan.

He was anxious to have this day end. His business was dealt with and now he wasn't doing much more than staring at the monitor and scrolling through his personal email. One of many Groupon posts showed *Charm City Helicopter Tours*. He had never heard of that. It dawned on him that it would be the perfect "wow factor" for after dinner Friday night. He wondered if he could still arrange the helicopter tour at sunset which would be the perfect event to end the day. He had figured on the Inner Harbor, but this could be much better. Way more "wow."

Rather than using the Groupon deal, since it was for the next day, he decided to call the tour company directly. A woman answered, "Hello Charm City Tours, how can I help you?"

"Hi, my name is Mike Bloom and it is my wife's birthday this weekend. I just got a Groupon email about your helicopter tours and I know it's last-minute but what time is your last flight tomorrow night and is there any chance we could get on it. There are four of us? Two are children."

"Slow down Mike, and happy birthday to your wife. Here's the deal. We just added back our eight o'clock flight on the first of May. Our summer hours. We haven't really advertised it yet, so tomorrow night is in fact, still open. And I can match the Groupon price. Call it a birthday gift." "Done," he said. He gave her a credit card to hold the reservation. In early May, that would put them in the air at dusk. Perfect. "The ride is twenty minutes, ten out and ten back," she said. "It will be one of the more memorable experiences you can have in Baltimore. Ask for Beth. Be here by seven-thirty if possible."

They would be in Baltimore by five-thirty, have an early dinner and then fly all around the city as lights were coming on. He was truly proud of himself. He was very excited about the start of the big weekend. After Washington, on Saturday they were to drop the kids off at his parents' home in Silver Spring and then Saturday night and Sunday morning were all for "Maggie and Mike." They would not rejoin the family until Mother's Day dinner scheduled for 2:00 pm with the grandparents.

After a nice lunch in Washington, food would not matter much on Saturday night. Sex would matter. Maggie is a fitness expert who came to Maryland at twenty-seven after working her way up at a fitness chain in Ohio. They were expanding and asked if she would make the move and become Assistant General Manager at their first Maryland studio along with the promise of her own studio to run when the expansion continued. She came, he joined. She smiled, he laughed. Suddenly, nearly thirteen years had passed. They had two kids, a manageable mortgage, and overall, a rather decent life. And she was still hot. A MILF, say our friends, not really in jest. Even now, as the General Manager of the Columbia location, she still taught some classes, practiced Yoga and Pilates and looked as good as the day he set eyes on her. He doesn't go to the gym much anymore. But he knows Maggie still thinks he's a hunk, and Saturday night he would try to prove it.

*****

On Friday morning he told Maggie that they were going to Sabatino's for dinner and taking the kids. She balked. "This better not be some well-intentioned birthday party where we walk in and twenty people pop up yelling surprise. I told you no fortieth birthday hoopla last year. I meant it then and mean it now!"

"Relax Maggie. It will be fun for the kids to go to Baltimore and enjoy Little Italy. If we eat early enough, we can go down to the Inner Harbor. You must let the kids make something of *your* birthday like you do for them." When it came to the kids, Maggie's priorities were set.

Jake and Annie loved the Inner Harbor, but Mike knew that after tonight they would know Baltimore in a new way and like it even more. At eleven and nine they were still young enough to enjoy playing in the city with their parents. In a few years as teenagers, they would be embarrassed by hanging out with Mom and Dad. But for the moment Maggie's birthday weekend would be better for having the kids involved as much as possible. Tonight would be fun for children of all ages.

*****

Sabatino's has been a joy and an icon throughout the lives of most Baltimore area residents. Its reputation is also such that visitors to town always seem to find their way over to Little Italy and the iconic restaurants there. It had been easy to get a reservation. Eating early has its benefits. He had mentioned to the hostess when he called that the occasion was the eve of his wife's birthday. They walked in right on time. Mike said, "Bloom for four." The woman at the desk smiled. "I'm Lisa, your hostess. I believe we spoke on the phone."

As Lisa led them to their table, she made a fuss over the kids. She then waved to a waiter, turned her head away so Maggie couldn't see, and mouthed "birthday" to him, hustling him to service. Maggie still seemed to be waiting for our friends to jump up and start singing. Could she be disappointed?

The atmosphere of white tablecloths, the smell of garlic and the clinking of wine glasses set the mood. The kids had buried their heads in the menu which read like a long homework assignment. The waiter approached. "Good evening everyone. I am Sal, and I'll be taking care of you this evening." He proceeded to rattle off an array of specials. Maggie simply smiled up at him and pro-ceeded to order. "We would like a large Bookmaker Salad, an order of garlic bread, and a carafe of the house Chianti. And Cokes for the kids." She knew the menu.

When the waiter returned with the wine and Cokes the kids were ready with their decision to share a Chicken Parma. Maggie ordered the Pasta special which was a Linguini with Crab Sauce, and Mike figured whatever he could not finish off an order of Sausage and Peppers would get shared among them or taken home. Little Annie had made it clear to him this morning that since we were not going to be at home doing a birthday cake, candles in Cannoli must happen for dessert. After they ordered, Annie excused herself to go to the bathroom. She then went down the hall to find Sal and give him instructions. She caught him coming out of the kitchen and tugged at his sleeve. "Sal, see my Mom over there." She subtly pointed back at the table. "This is my mom's birthday dinner." She reached into her pocket and removed two candles. A four and a one. "Please put these into whatever dessert she orders. Put them in backward so it says fourteen. Mom would rather laugh than admit to forty-one." Annie was taking charge and knew what to do, just like the little Maggie she was.

*****

Mike pulled the car into a parking space at the pier just as the sun was dropping behind the buildings of downtown. There was still light in the sky and the last rays of the sun were streaming off the body and blades of the only thing sitting out on the pier. A helicopter. Maggie gasped. "Oh my God Mike. Now what? We're not going up in that!"

Mike laughed. "Of course, we are, darling. Why do you think we ate dinner so early? We were on a tight schedule. We are going on the last flight of the evening at eight o'clock and see the city as it lights up"

"Mike, you've lost your mind. Really, Mike, I think this is——"Suddenly the rear door burst open and Jake was out of the car racing up the pier. His sister not far behind. "Hold that thought Mags. This will be fun. Don't be a spoilsport," he quipped. "Let's go. It's getting dark."

Leading up to her birthday last year, she had told him over and over she did not want to make a big deal about turning forty. No party, please. She said, "I'm thirty-nine now. I want to stay thirty-nine on my birthday, and I may wish to be thirty-nine again on my next birthday." Forty was a big deal to Maggie. Mike remembered a couple of months before her birthday they were at the fortieth birthday party of one of her friends, Julie Dobbs. Julie had a third child at thirty-nine. On her birthday cake was written, *"I'd Rather Be Forty Than Pregnant."* Maggie had given Mike a look which told him not to try and add any additional humor. But after Maggie's fortieth birthday passed, it felt wrong that he had done virtually nothing. Do women always mean what they say? Doubtful. He felt he blew it. This time he was going to make it right. All he wanted was a Sunday night kiss and hearing her say, "Wow Mike, that was a great weekend."

As the helicopter lifted off the pier Mike had the sensation that he had left something behind on the ground. Something internal. As Jake and Annie yelped with glee, Maggie was whispering in his ear, "Mike this is on you. I never liked flying; you recall." As they rose and leveled-off, they swooped over toward Camden Yards. It was lit up for a night game. It looked magnificent from the sky. The grass, the lights and the slightest hint of movement on the field. The kids pointed this way and that at the various sites, at the same time they looked terrified. Fort McHenry was softly lit by low accent lighting. Maggie looked a bit green. Across the city, the buildings and the harbor lights were just coming on as dusk turned to dark. Mike was only slightly less uncomfortable. Beautiful, but he still fought the urge to close his eyes. It was truly a magnificent view of Charm City. Maggie and Mike seemed to relax and enjoy the view just in time for the helicopter to circle back and head toward the pier. After the hard tilt and turn, Annie shrieked like she was on a roller coaster. Jake looked unearthly calm. They were all grinning ear to ear as the bird (pilot's word in our headset) hovered and gently sat itself down on the pier, bringing on group applause.

When they got back into the car, they were all looking a bit peaked but there were also smiles. Mike for one, was thrilled to be back on the ground. "Dad," Jake said, "that was the coolest thing I've ever done. Do you think I could learn to fly one of those *birds*?" Annie was a bit less enthusiastic. "Dad, you do remember that Mom and I are afraid of heights?" Mike gulped as Maggie gave him the glare, the one he'd been both expecting and dreading. He was instantly saved by Annie continuing to say, "But I agree with Jake, that was awesome." They were both fast asleep in the car before they got home. A good thing too. They were all leaving at nine a.m. sharp for the Nation's Capital.

*****

Mike and his family stood outside on the steps to the Lincoln Memorial. The sky was azure, and the sunshine was rapidly warming the cool overnight air. He had just received a text from Harris saying, *"Can't make this morning. see you this afternoon."* Shortly, Josh was striding up the path and waving them all around to the side of the Memorial. Mike's family followed along to the side steps where they went down to a steel door. By the time they descended he had a key in the lock. The door squealed when he opened it. Josh reached in and flipped on a low wattage light over the entryway. As they all shuffled in behind him, they saw construction scaffolding and ladders in every direction.

Annie spoke first. "What's that smell?" "Time" Josh replied. "This place had been locked up nearly thirty years and for nearly 100 years has been a basement of sorts. Follow me and watch your step." Josh flicked the switch on a powerful flashlight. Scaffolding surrounded most of the walls. In front of them stood concrete pillars which obviously held up the floor of the Memorial above. Strong enough to support a giant of a man sitting in his chair. Stairs descended in from of them. Josh waved the family to follow him.

"Careful, watch your step," he said. Jake was engrossed. "Hey Dad, look at all the graffiti." While pointing the flashlight all around, Josh said, "There are drawings and cartoons all over the walls and pillars. The workers in 1914 did not have portable music players or even radio. When they got bored or were on lunch break, they drew or wrote on the walls."

They got to the bottom of the stairs and began walking on a railed walkway. Josh pointed the flashlight upward. "Look at the stalactites." Then he said, "Watch for motion." Insects and rodents scattered to avoid the light. As they continued Josh pointed out the viewing area which was under construction. Maggie was poking her husband in the back and whispered that maybe Annie needed a bathroom. What Annie said, however, was, "Dad, can we get out of here? This place gives me the creeps." You've got to love a kid who always speaks her mind. They retraced their steps back toward the entry door. Thanked Josh profusely. It was only twenty minutes of being underground but the sunshine and blue sky were a welcome sight. A memorable visit for certain, but surely lacking in charm. Maybe they'd come back when the renovations were done and the Undercroft open again.

*****

Their next stop, before they were to meet up with Harris at the Mansion at two o'clock, was lunch at the Old Ebbitt Grill. A DC landmark with a great atmosphere and very good food. Mike had invited Josh to join but he begged off, claiming many family errands to run on a Saturday. Mike figured he did not want to horn in on Maggie's birthday lunch. Mike had parked the car on a street up near Dupont Circle and they had Uber'd to the Monuments. It was barely eleven and too early for lunch. It was a beautiful spring day and they decided there was plenty of time to walk along the Reflecting Pool, look at the World War II Memorial – a war which Jake had been studying in school and had talked with his grandfather about – and then pass by the Washington Monument and act like the tourists they were today. Then they would head up 15th St. to the restaurant.

Maggie once again took charge of ordering. She and her girlfriends came to the Ebbitt whenever they ventured to town to go to the museums. She ordered two Double Crab Cake platters and a Mixed Green Salad to share first. She paused; the waiter focused on Maggie waiting for more. She turned and winked at Mike and then said, "And how about you bring out two dozen oysters as an appetizer." Mike imagined she was thinking that oysters could lead to an evening where he might be the main course. Mike's smile got bigger. Annie scrunched up her face and cringed. "How can you eat those slimy things."

At this point, Maggie was glowing. They had all walked much of the way holding hands and creating a roadblock on the sidewalk. Maggie and Mike in the middle, Jake holding Maggie's right hand and Annie holding Mike's left. When they were smaller, they would insist on being swung back and forth in the middle. Little babies one minute and then so big they couldn't be lifted.

Everything was delicious. When all the plates had been cleared, the waiter returned and asked if they wanted coffee or dessert. Just as Maggie was about to say, "no thank you," a server walked up behind him with a large Brownie Sundae with one candle aflame. Several other staff joined him. They began singing "Happy Birthday." It was perfect. This weekend celebration would likely lead to Maggie insisting they go on a diet and workout regimen. Stuffed to the gills, they were back in an Uber heading uptown to Dupont Circle and the Mansion on O St. When they pulled up, Harris was waiting on the sidewalk.

Harris started with, "Sorry to bail on you this morning. I do children's music. You know, play guitar and sing songs that four-year old's giggle at. Got a last-minute call to fill in when the regular Saturday guy got sick." He still seemed very excited about showing off the Mansion, which, he repeated, was both, a hotel and a museum. "I met the owners a while back and when they found out what I did in the music business they called on me for help with this and that. I love this place. The owners are very special."

Being a Saturday, they were open for tours anyway. But Harris waved them down a few steps to a door. He entered a code and they came in at the bottom of a narrow staircase. A man stepped out of the room on the right and gave Harris a big hug. He was introduced to them as Ted. He was the President of the hotel and museum. His wife was the founder. From that moment on everything was a blur. Total sensory overload. Ted explained that they were in five connected row houses. There were over one hundred rooms, nearly as many chandeliers. There were exotic art and collectibles, private guest rooms throughout the maze of stairways and doorways. It was apparently a haven, and many famous people had stayed, and even lived, at the fabulous hotel. Everything there had been donated and was for sale in support of the enterprise. Then Ted looked down at Jake and Annie. "Last, but not least, there are seventy secret doors. Start your tour and keep count of how many you find."

Maggie and Mike saw their children only twice in the next two hours as they wandered up, down and across the five houses. There is no narrative to describe what they saw. People simply need to visit for themselves. When they finally went out the front door Harris was grinning from ear to ear, "What'd you think? Pretty amazing, huh."

Maggie reached over and gave him a hug. "Harris, you don't even know me, and you still produced the most amazing birthday present ever. I can't wait to show this to people who've never been here." Over her shoulder, he looked at Mike and winked. Mike mouthed "thanks" and gave him a thumbs up. Maggie said, "Harris, let us know when you'll be at the club in Columbia again. We will both come next time. You have a new fan."

*****

The weekend had been more than a mild success so far. Now that they had dropped the children off at his parents they had until tomorrow afternoon when the Mother's Day meal was planned. It was "Maggie" time. He thought to himself, oysters do your thing, hoping it was not a myth. It was just after seven o'clock when the Thai food arrived. Mike went to the door, accepted the delivery, tipped the driver and was just placing the bag of food on the kitchen counter when he heard Maggie call from the bedroom, "Mike could you come in here a minute? "He walked into the bedroom and nearly stumbled it was so dark. There were four candles lit on the dresser and one on the nightstand. On the dresser, an open bottle of wine with two glasses already poured. Dark red, inviting, and sultry. As his eyes adjusted to the dim light, he saw Maggie slip out of the bathroom and fold herself onto the bed. She was undressed and as beautiful as the first time he saw her naked body. The first time was on their second date. It was the last date Mike ever had. It has been just Maggie ever since. She had used her fitness career to stay looking younger than her age. He turned and picked up both glasses of wine and walked over to the bed and handed one to her. He held up the other and proposed a toast. "To the most beautiful woman I have ever known, and ever will know, the mother of my children, the keeper of the flame. I love you, birthday girl." The clothing Mike was wearing seemed to evaporate. They each took a strong gulp of wine. He crawled in beside her. The sounds in the room were no longer words.

It was after eleven p.m. and they were curled up, still naked under the covers, each with a bowl of reheated Pad Thai on their lap. Mike smiled. "You seem a bit flushed Maggie dear, too much cardio?" Maggie laughed, never ashamed of her passion, looked him dead in the eye. "No Mike, too much Siracha."

*****

Mike awoke in a tangle of sheets. The morning sun was creeping through the curtains. The remainder of last night a bit of a blur. They had washed down the Thai food with the rest of the red wine. That bottle stood empty on the dresser across the room. It was the two shot glasses on the nightstand and the empty bottle of Sambuca Mike saw lying on its side on the floor beside the bed that gradually brought Mike to some clarity. They had been refueled with food and her lips had tasted so good and so sweet from the Sambuca. He snuggled up to Maggie and watched her eyelids flutter awake. She smiled up at him and began to slip out of bed. He grinned. "Happy Mother's Day, mother of my children. Children who are not in the house this morning that is." He went to pull her back into bed, thinking morning sex was the way to start the day. Maggie, moving like a cat, was already out of bed and dancing toward the bathroom. She spun around, unabashedly naked and laughing. "You have ravaged me adequately for my birthday and ordinarily I would jump your bones on a Sunday with the house to ourselves, but I am totally sated for the moment and do I need to remind you, Mother's Day morning you said you would do whatever I asked." Mike frowned and began to wish he had held that promise until this morning and thus would have had time for it to be given proper assessment. "I," she said, "have turned forty-one, middle-aged, and I need to maintain this body you love so much. And you sir, adorable as you are, seemed a bit more taxed than a man in good shape should be. You have two choices. We go to the gym or we take a long bike ride." Mike hated the gym. Especially, being the out of shape husband of the boss. "How long a bike ride," he asked, a bit sheepishly.

Still able to maintain some Mother's Day morning rituals, Maggie had climbed back into bed after what seemed an eternity in the bathroom. Mike had cleaned up the glasses and dead soldiers from the night before and set a tray across her lap. An egg, over easy on a half English Muffin, cut up strawberries and blackberries, and a coffee with foamed milk. He had had his coffee and the other half of the muffin while putting Maggie's breakfast together.

"Mike, you know how much I love to be spoiled like this. The weekend has been wonderful. You and the kids have outdone yourselves. Now, while I enjoy this wonderful breakfast, please go get cleaned up and ready to ride."

****

Maggie reached over and pressed the garage door opener. Mike, in spandex bike shorts, a white t-shirt and black helmet, rolled his bike out first. As Maggie came out behind him, he hit the outside button to close the door. She was down the driveway and speeding off down the street as he mounted his bike. "Come on pokey," she called out over her shoulder.

They had now been riding for over an hour. Around the neighborhoods, through the parks, and were taking a water break in the shade of a large Oak. "Did you have breakfast?" she asked. He shrugged. "Had coffee and a muffin." She replied, "You must be starved after all this exercise. Let's ride down toward the lake and go to the café. I'll race you. Last one there buys." Competitive Maggie stowed her water bottle, jumped back on her bike and took off. Mike did the same and was quickly pedaling in her wake. He rode hard and at the bottom of a hill, Mike flew by her. By the time they came down the main street by the lake, Maggie was a hundred yards behind him. Mike was straining to keep up the pace and the lead. She had the endurance, but he had the speed.

Thinking to himself, unlike last night, on a bike he was a sprinter. He looked over his shoulder to try to catch a glimpse of her bright blue helmet. Before he could turn his head forward, there was an impact and he was going down hard. "Shit," he thought, as something soft seemed to crack beneath him. Not something. Someone. He was dazed and could not entangle himself from the bike which had pinned both he and an older woman down to the street. The woman cried out in pain. Mike was disoriented. "Oh my god, are you okay? Don't try to move."

Suddenly a policeman was hoisting him up. Maggie pulled up on her bike. Seeing on her face a look of horror and disbelief, he uttered, "I'm sorry Mags. We nearly made it through a perfect weekend. Happy Mother's Day, anyway." At their feet, a slender woman with long gray hair moaned softly.

Fun references:

https://www.thesoundry.com/

https://sabatinos.com/

https://flycharmcity.com/

https://www.atlasobscura.com/places/lincoln-memorial-undercroft

https://www.ebbitt.com/

https://omansion.com/

MINGO FISHTRAP 2005

"Oh, please Liz I really want to go." Mark had not stopped begging her to go on the music cruise thing. These guys he knew at the University of North Texas back in the 90s had become a band. They were starting to get some traction and were playing on the *Delbert McClinton Sandy Beaches* music cruise for the first time. The cruises had begun in 1995 and had grown into a line-up of Austin's finest and more. Finally, early next year, January 2005, *Mingo Fishtrap* was booked to go on the cruise along with over twenty other acts including *Delbert, Marcia Ball, John Hiatt,* and many more notables. Virtually Texas royalty and other stars. She got that. It would leave Fort Lauderdale on the 8th and go island hopping for a week. He explained, "The music starts late morning, multiple stages, goes past midnight. Then they jam in the lounges until near daybreak. It has got to be a blast."

The real reason Mark was so desperate to go on the trip was, that he had dreamed of being the bass player in that band. They were all music majors in college when the band had formed. Relegated to just being one of their biggest fans, he was jazzed about them being on the cruise this year. Although the band was formed at the University of North Texas, they had moved downstate and become Austin-based. The irony of not being considered for being the bass player in the band came from an odd moment in time, back in the 1990s, when their regular bass player did not show up for a gig. "Coincidentally," Mark told Liz, "Roger Blevins Jr, the lead singer in the band, had his father, Roger Sr., paying a visit that weekend. Being that his dad was a professional touring bass player he learned some songs and sat in, end of the story. To this day Roger Sr. is still the Mingo Fishtrap bass player and I'm not." She gave him a blank look. He renewed his pitch.

"Come on Liz you can take a week off. Mom says that you haven't smiled since the divorce. Truthfully, she said you hadn't smiled for the entire last year you were married. Don't you think it's time to get back to your life? You're only twenty-five. Your life is not over. I'll come up and we can fly from Dallas."

Mark was four years older than Liz and rather transparent. He was married, had a young son, and his wife, Helen, was seven months pregnant with their second. Liz knew she had already vetoed any notion of going on a rowdy music cruise. Helen had called to prepare her for the onslaught. She said she told him, "Mark Tanner, I am not dumping the baby on your mom in Denton, flying to Florida, squeezing oversize me in an undersized cabin just to watch you drink and party for a week. You do understand that, right? Been there, done that!"

That part was true. Four years ago, when Mark was engaged to Helen, he had taken her on Sandy Beaches #7. They had flown to Tampa on New Year's Day and sailed the next day. It was like nothing they had ever imagined. The music started on the first evening. Helen said she went back to the cabin around midnight. Mark came back who knows when. He would catch as much sleep as possible between four am and nine or so, eat breakfast and be ready for the first morning-show around eleven. And on throughout the week it went, stage after stage across the boat. Helen did not complain and admitted it was great for the music, if not for their relationship. She then laughed and told Liz, "I was really in love with Mark and married him anyway." Once they were back home it was all just a memory. But not again. This time it was talk Liz into going, or not go. Helen had shared, "I told him there was no way I'd approve of him going with any of his drinking buddies either, then I told him to invite you. Sorry about that, Sis. It seemed like a good idea at the time."

Liz continued to be a hard sell. "I haven't been with the Morning News very long. Do you think I can just up and ask for a week off?"

"Yeah, I do," he said. "And you know they wouldn't bat an eye about saying yes." Mark and Helen had come up to visit Mom right after Liz had moved to Dallas for the job. They went to a party with Liz and mainly newspaper staffers and had met Liz's boss, Al Grant. He was very open with Mark. He said, "Liz is our new superstar. She's a great journalist with a big future. I worry a bit about her though. She seems a bit shell shocked. Do you think it's the divorce?" Mark knew what he was saying. "Maybe a bit," he said. "More disappointed in her choices than unhappy about it. She always thought she knew everything. Angry at herself for the waste of time it turned out to be. They were near graduation after dating for over two years. She could not see beyond them being together, so they got married. They were happy for a minute."

Al smiled. "You really look out for her, don't you?" Mark nodded. "That's good," Al said. "Her work is fine. She just needs to relax a bit. If she needs some time off, I'd support it."

Armed with that knowledge Mark pushed a bit harder and Liz relented. "Dammit Mark, I'll go if only to stop you from being a bigger asshole about it. Just tell me you are over "*not being in the band*." Tell me we can just hang out, listen to music, and chill. Then tell me you'll get me the unlimited alcohol package and I don't have to pay, all your treat, and we can be done here." She even wound up promising Al an article for the paper, saying, "No problem, boss, assuming I remember anything." Mark booked plane tickets for the morning of January 8th, Dallas to Fort Lauderdale. Then, they would be shuttled directly to the port and board the ship.

*****

The transport bus drove down a long pier with several large cruise ships docked end to end. As they pulled up to the Holland America ms Zuiderdam they were relieved to see it was one of the smaller ships. Likely around two thousand passengers rather than the monster boats which hold four or five thousand. The driver told them that the boat was still rather new. On the water, less than five years. Mark had booked a cabin with a verandah. He expected his sister might need to be able to separate a bit. An outdoor space might be the "breath of fresh air" required to make the accommodations truly accommodating. They queued up to show their paperwork, tickets, passports, etc. Their luggage was taken away, to be delivered to their deck and placed outside their cabin door. Most startling as they proceeded to the boarding ramps was the massive quantity of musical equipment. Cases holding instruments and gear were stacked ten to twenty feet high and across an entire wall. It took quite a while to board the ship. Corridors and ramps, then an elevator to the cabin deck.

They beat their luggage to the cabin. Mark opened the door with a key card. Bright sunshine was streaming in from the slider out to the balcony. In the middle of the room was a queen-sized bed.

Liz choked out, "Ah, Mark, I have no intention of sleeping in the same bed as you. We are not little kids anymore. Last time, I may have been six and you kicked me all night." "No worries," he said. "It sets up as twins. I saw it on the website. I must have missed checking the box on the registration. Let's go find housekeeping and ask them to change it."

"Nah, let's just do it ourselves. I'm whipped. Been up since five a.m. I just want to crash until that '*welcome thing*' late this afternoon." She grabbed the bedspread and ripped it off. Then pulled up the queen sheets to re-veal a pad that laid across to cover the split. She yanked that off, kneed her way between the two halves, pushed one bed one way, turned and shoved the other away. "Shit, we don't have the sheets for twin beds. You better call housekeeping after all." Exasperated, she uttered, "I'm out of here." She whirled to the door, waved, "If you need me, I'm going to find a bar."

*****

She was angry at herself for being pissy to Mark. Again. Not the first time since he talked her into this. She had promised herself to leave it on land. Maybe still being tied to the dock counts as that. Chill, girl. He is right, she needed this trip. Take deep breaths. Get rid of the anger. Her anger, self-directed of course, even if she tended to take it out on her brother. The aft deck bar was open for business and more than half the stools were already occupied. She grabbed one with an open stool on each side. Crapshoot. Two possibilities of a single guy sliding up next to her. It was nearly two o'clock and she was hungry as well as thirsty. A cute thirty-something bartender appeared and slapped down a coaster. "Welcome aboard young lady, what will it be?" She smiled back, may have even batted an eye, but involuntarily. "A Mojito and a menu would be great. Thank you."

"I'm sorry miss. We don't serve food here at the bar. I can offer you peanuts or pretzels with your drink. Or, I'll hold your seat if you want to walk down to the marketplace dining area and bring something back." "That's sweet," she said. "But I'll save the walk, for now, thanks. I'll have two Mojitos. One with peanuts and one with pretzels."

It did not take long for the barstool to Liz's right to be filled. As Liz looked over, she noted the guy was cute in a mature, slightly graying way. He called the bartender over and ordered vodka rocks. He then swiveled the stool toward her and said, "Hi I'm Mitch. And you are? "He had a nice smile and a little devil in his eye. She replied, "I'm Liz." He wore no wedding band and began flirting immediately. She figured she'd have another Mojito and see what happens. After all, she was on this boat to have some fun. And she had not been with a man in a long time. Long before the divorce, that part of her marriage had ended. She and Mitch swapped stories a bit. He said he was from Atlanta and was a vice-president of the company that rented all the gear for the bands. Amps, speakers, boards, etc. Whatever is needed to put on the show. The company always had to have one executive on board for goodwill and relationship building. This year was his turn. This was a good customer for his company and a great perk for him. She told him she had just moved up from Austin to the Dallas Morning News. "I'm a journalist. Metro Desk." Further, she said, "I was divorced last year. I'm here to drink and have some fun. You know, blow off some steam. Get my Mojo back."

Nothing had really happened except that at some point Mitch had put his arm on her shoulder and then dropped it to her waist. She had leaned in and draped her right arm across his shoulder while bringing up her left hand about to take a sip of her Mojito. Suddenly, a vicious scream from behind her.

"Get your hands off my husband. "

A short brunette with teased hair and a sneer pulled Liz's arm off Mitch's shoulder and continued her tirade. "Tramp" she yelled, as she gave Liz an evil eye. Then she turned it on Mitch., "You son of a bitch! You come down to the bar after telling me I should take a nap. Then you start groping the first pretty young thing you can find. What was next, a quickie in her cabin before I woke up?"

Liz was mortified. "I was not doing anything with your husband. We were just having a drink. He had no ring. I just assumed——" The blonde raised her voice another notch. "Ring? Mitchell, you asshole. I should have known it was bullshit when you said the ring was bothering your golf grip. I'll bet you've been cruising bars all over Atlanta." Suddenly she burst into tears.

Mark

Mark had just entered the bar looking for Liz when he heard the screaming. He heard "hands off my husband" and "tramp" and "quickie" and saw a screaming woman directing her attack on Liz. Oh no. Now what? He quickly assessed the situation and decided. He stepped to the bar and came up behind Liz. "Darling, thanks for waiting for me." Then he turned toward the woman. "Why are you yelling at my wife? What the hell do you think she was doing? I was only gone a few minutes and she certainly had no interest in your husband. You have no cause to be screaming at her." At which point he grabbed Liz's hand, pulled her off the stool, put his arm around her, and marched her out of the bar leaving Mitch and his wife to battle it out.

Back at the cabin getting ready for the welcome event Liz turned to Mark and laughed, "Thanks for the save. "But, wife, that's a rich one." He replied, "What did you want me to do? Let that guy's wife tear your head off for pawing her husband? How would that have played out? Admit it, Sis, I bailed you out without any further embarrassment. It's a big boat. Lots of people. You are probably still anonymous. Flirt all you want, just be careful of these married guys"

"Sure Mark. Married guys are all dogs. My ex surely was. I'll remind Helen when we get back."

"That is not fair, Lizzy. You know I've never cheated on Helen. I'm here for the music, and up to a point, you should be too. Let it wash over you and lift your spirits. That's what good music does. Let's get up on deck and see the first show. Delbert and friends will be on in five."

*****

Liz had to admit, the next several days were awesome. She tried to keep up with her brother all day but eventually, she would just crash. They ran from one stage to another. The outdoor main stage on deck was created by covering over one of the large pools. That made the entire rear of the boat like a festival ground with balconies along the sides. The bow of the ship housed a large theater. The Mainstage is what they called it. It seemed to seat over 1000 people. Other lounges and atriums also housed stages. It was John Hiatt here and then scamper to the other end of the ship and see Canadians such as Fred Eaglesmith and Colin Linden. Back and forth, up and down. Drinking, smoking weed, and eating as much as they wanted. She fell in love with Paul Thorn and Randall Bramblett. This guy Russell Smith started singing and it took her back to her childhood. Smith had been the lead singer in her Dad's favorite seventies group, *The Amazing Rhythm Aces.* She never knew his name but the minute he started singing the voice popped in her head. Mark had been right. This much music in such intimate surroundings was soothing her soul. Some artists made her laugh, others made her cry, but through it all, the music put joy in the heart and satisfied her mind, so she thought of little else.

*****

By Tuesday it was time for the first Mingo Fishtrap set. Mark was excited. "Liz," he said, "I want to get right next to the soundboard for them. The sound guy is Gabe. I've met him a few times. Nice guy. He said if I hung close and reminded him, he would make me a copy of their set. He has a CD burner set up and he was making one for himself anyway." Ten minutes before showtime, they had parked themselves on the edge of the platform riser the soundboard was on. And guess what, Gabe was indeed a handsome guy in a hardscrabble sort of way. Under six feet with broad shoulders, medium length messy hair, beard cut to stubble, shorts, flip flops and a black t-shirt that promoted Austin City Limits.

"Hi Gabe," Liz said when Mark introduced her. "She's with me," Mark said. "Okay if she hangs here?"

Gabe looked her over and seemed to like what he saw. "That's fine Mark, there is plenty of room for both of you."

Once the set began Gabe's attention was on his job and Mark wandered off saying he wanted to listen from various places. Gabe rarely even looked down. Liz, on the other hand, glanced up quite a bit. He was adorable. The band was great too. Really great. The crowd was totally into it. Much like her recollection of her trip to JazzFest in New Orleans when she was eighteen. The music seemed to merge people of all types into one heart and one mind, if only for a few minutes. When the set ended the crew and the band milled about for a few minutes. Gabe was packing up. Liz stayed close. Made small talk. Mark came back over. "Hey Liz, the guys are going to party down in the forward lounge. Do you want to come?"

"No thanks, Mark, I think I'll just hang here and talk to Gabe a bit more. I'll catch up later."

Mark smiled, gave Gabe a "thumbs up" and said, "Good idea. Have fun."

Liz and Gabe hung out at the deck bar a while and had several drinks. She lost count after the first two Tequila shots. Gabe said, "With everybody at the party nobody will be in my cabin for a while. Would you like to come down for a bit? I'd feel better in my cabin than yours if you get my drift."

Liz was not sure what he meant, but he was sexy as hell and she was hornier than she realized. "I would like that very much" she replied. They headed down the stairs to deck six where the band crew was housed. Gabe opened the door to his cabin and just as he had said, it was deserted. They sat down on the bed together and kicked their shoes off. They leaned into each other and almost giggled. She felt a quickening as he leaned over and gave her a gentle kiss. She kissed him back harder. She could feel her blood coming up. It had been a long time. He unbuttoned her blouse then reached around behind her feeling for her the hooks on the bra strap. He deftly undid the hook and swept his hand under and around to her breast. He pulled his head back and looked her in the eye.

Then he said, "it's really "cool" that Mark lets you do this. Do you have an open marriage, or did you guys just decide to mess around on the cruise?"

"He lets me!! Prowl? What the hell are you talking about!!" Liz barked as she closed her blouse around herself and jumped up.

"Well," Gabe uttered, "it's going around the boat that Mark pulled his wife away from a scene in the bar. They are saying that you were coming on to a married guy when the guy's wife walked in. I just assumed you were looking to get laid."

"Oh my God," said Liz. "I can't believe it. Mark is my brother, you idiot. He saw some woman yelling at me for something I didn't do. It had been harmless, and the guy acted single and he was seriously flirting with me. My brother walked in and heard the commotion, so he came over and took me out of an embarrassing situation saying I was his wife and he had been there the whole time. I thought the band knew I was his sister. Yuk! You thought you were going to sleep with his wife, you asshole? That really creeps me out."

"Oh shit," Gabe said. "I guess they didn't tell me. I'm so sorry Liz. Thinking what I was thinking, I simply thought that I had gotten lucky with a hot married chick."

Liz reached around and reattached her bra strap. She then finished buttoning her blouse and turned back to Gabe. "This hot chick did want you, and my body still wants you, but you turned out to be a guy who would sleep with someone's wife after patting him on the back an hour ago."

The walls shook when Liz slammed the cabin door on her way out. She made a beeline back up the stairs to her cabin deck. She just wanted to get inside and lock the door. Unsure whether to laugh or cry, somewhere between anger and humiliation. How the hell had a rumor about what happened in the bar gotten around to the bands? If she knew that, both she and Mark could have defused it as the joke that it was. Funny then, not so funny now.

The hall was quiet. The evening parties had evaporated into the big nightly show in the theater in the bow. Liz found her room, inserted the key card, slipped inside and plopped face down on her bed. A fly on the wall would have heard a string of muffled curses mixed with sobs being buried in the pillow. Several minutes went by when suddenly Liz rolled over and sat bolt upright. Straight ahead, against the wall, was the minibar. Salvation came in three tiny bottles of Jack Daniels. The first took it all down a notch. The second brought a small smile, bordering on a grin. Two hits off the joint she had stowed in her make-up case and she was much more relaxed. By the time she twisted the little metal screw cap off the third bottle she had scooted her butt onto the pillow and was leaning back using the wall for support. Liz then said to the empty room, "Did I over-react?" She began to replay the entire scene in her mind. She stopped short and backed the story up. Then, Liz continued aloud, "Maybe I should look at this from Gabe's perspective."

And she did. Gabe clearly heard through the grapevine that Mark had called her his wife. And it was in the context of a bar pickup gone wrong when the guy's wife showed up. Then Mark parked her by the soundboard, virtually asking Gabe to keep her company, and wandered away leaving her to flirt with him. The Mingo Fishtrap show ends, Mark heads out to hang with the band and she says, "I think I'll just hang here with Gabe a bit." If Liz allows herself to think as Gabe may have, he likely believed that she was coming on to him and that it was alright with Mark. Thinking as Gabe, she sees how it changed everything. Neither expected a relationship. Gabe certainly did not. He thought she was married. Liz was honestly just seeking a fling in order to get back in the game, not to mention the sex. Liz closed her eyes and somewhere between awake and asleep, she replayed the scene another way. In her dream, she heard, *"You are so pretty and so sexy and I thought you were hitting on me. Please, can we start this over? Hi, my name is Gabe, what's yours?"*

*****

When Liz reluctantly opened her eyes early the next morning, the barest amount of daylight was peeking around the curtain on the sliding glass door. It was still enough to cause her headache to rise as well. She was covered with a light blanket but was still in her clothes. Mark was in his bed with the blanket pulled up over his head and was snoring quietly. She vaguely remembered Mark coming in late. Two something according to the clock on the bedside table. He gently had tried to wake her. Mark then whispered, "I've told everyone I know that you're my sister. I practically made an announcement. Gabe came and told me what happened. He was so ashamed of himself. Mostly because he had acted like sleeping with my wife was okay. Jerk."

Those were the last words Liz recalled him saying before she fell back to sleep. Coming fully awake and sitting up she felt the makings of a full-blown hangover. There were quite a few more little liquor bottles on the dresser than she recalled opening. Vodka had joined the Jack Daniels at some point. Coffee, now! She quietly got up and thought to change her shirt to look less like she slept in her clothes. She slipped out the cabin door to head for the breakfast buffet. As she climbed the stairs to the main deck, last night rolled around in her head. The way she was angered at first. Storming out. Rethinking the whole mess. Mark being cavalier on Sunday in the bar. She, playing the fool on Tuesday. Gabe, both the foil and the dupe. He was so sweet and good-looking but, no, he must be a jerk. Or maybe not? What the hell. Three more days on the water to find out.

Liz was on her second cup of coffee when Mark sauntered in, showered and looking fresh as a daisy. He was as chipper as Liz was glum. "Hi there, sis. You look a bit worse for wear. It's not that bad. From what I understand you didn't go very far before it became a total embarrassment."

Liz replied, "I guess that's a good thing, but now I'm both horny and miserable."

"Well, I have something positive to tell you," he said with a shit-eating grin. "Last night at the party I ran into Danny Black. He is on the boat tour managing for a couple of the Austin bands. Must be doing it for kicks because he said he was a teacher, and not in Austin, but in Dallas. You might remember him. We went to high school together. He came by the house a lot. Good looking. Played shortstop on the baseball team. You were twelve or thirteen. Funny how he used to say that my little sister was going to be a man-eater when she grew up. He got very flustered when I told him you were on the trip. He's been divorced for nearly three years. You two are perfect for each other. Go get cleaned up. I told him I'd ring his cabin and we'd all have lunch before the first set started."

Liz looked at him like he was crazy. "Wow, Mark to the rescue again. In your head I am going to meet Danny, fall in love, go back to Dallas and move in together, just like that. Nice fantasy big brother. Dream on, dreamer."

Mark retorted, "Fine Liz, I get it. You may not be the romantic you once were. Of course not. Who is? Life has its ups and downs. But lunch with Danny is harmless and has the potential to put this Gabe thing behind you. So why not?"

Liz got up to leave, go back to the cabin to shower and make herself presentable. As she walked away, she spun around and winked. "Gabe who?"

Fun references:

https://www.mingofishtrap.com/

https://sandybeachescruises.com/home+

JAMAL'S STORY

When Jamal was discharged from the Army, he felt like he needed to be somewhere familiar. He had been orphaned at a Baltimore city hospital and raised by the foster care system. After high school, he could not wait to leave. He had played football and had done well. He might even have gotten a college scholarship. His coach had been supportive, but at that moment in time, Jamal was glad to be done with school. After trying a few dead-end jobs, he felt that joining the military would be the quickest way to move on with his life. He also figured that if he didn't get himself killed, he would be all the better for the experience and would have more options than a foster kid on the streets of Baltimore at nineteen. He had grown up on the streets as a way of life. Mainly to avoid going home to a foster parent who was only in it for the money and could not define nurture with a dictionary opened to the page it was on. That chapter of his life was over. He was not a kid anymore. He had spent eight years in the Army, much of the time as Military Police. When his first six-year stint was up he signed on for another two which allowed him to save more money for his re-entry to civilian life. He had no family to return to and thus no support would be offered by anyone. The

Army had been his family since high school. At twenty-seven he was truly on his own for the first time.

He watched cop shows growing up because his foster mom at the time was addicted to them all. *Hill Street Blues*, and all the older ones with reruns on all day long. She especially liked *Homicide, Life on the Streets*, which took place in Baltimore. Jamal had a friend in the service, Max Holland, who, when he had gotten out went on to study at a community college. Whenever Jamal touched base with him, he would rave on about what a good decision it was. It was made affordable by Army benefits and he kept saying, "It put him on the path to success." He usually sounded like he had been drinking the Kool-Aid. But Jamal remembered how positive he was and decided to go speak to a counselor at the county community college.

When he met with the counselor, Ms. Stafford, her name, according to the placard facing him across the desk, she kept coming back to his background as an MP. "Jamal," she said, "You might pursue a career in Criminal Justice. The college is currently hiring additional security officers as their response to gun violence which has spread to both high school and college campuses across the country. You could apply for that job now while taking classes. As an employee, your academic cost would be minimal. Then, with your background and some college work, you would be a good candidate to apply to the Howard County Police Department. Does that sound like something you would be interested in?"

What happened next seemed inevitable. He signed up for classes, got the security job and tapped his army savings to rent an apartment in Ellicott City.

Jamal didn't spend much time thinking about why he was an abandoned child. Why he, as a baby, was left in the hospital emergency room under a chair, and then put into a system that barely provided for his needs. But somehow, he survived. His faith did not come from organized religion. His exposure to that had been sporadic at best. Some of the foster parents were devout and others not. He didn't accept the idea of creation since what he saw in the natural world had so obviously evolved. He believed in the scientific world. To him, science explained most everything. Jamal understood organized religion as something that was founded at a time where grand questions could not be answered, and fears could not be quelled without something to hold onto. In nature, he could see that "survival of the fittest" was a hard truth. Certainly, his truth. Science showed him why rivers flow in a certain direction, how instinctive it was that animals would fear danger, hunt for food and seek shelter. Much the same, their human counterparts need those same things. Jamal wanted to be a man who was pragmatic and a realist. His education would come in support of his army discipline and make it so. He hoped.

After looking over the curriculum for his Criminal Justice major, Jamal learned that he would need to satisfy arts and sciences electives by taking courses in philosophy and sociology. He quickly decided to avoid them in the first year. Jamal imagined those course topics would take him to a place inside himself that he had long ago tried to shut down. The "why" of his past. As he matured and looked at the experiences he had as a military policeman and to appreciate his current choices, he began to live for the future. Not dwell on the past.

An incident that occurred less than a month or so into Jamal's tenure as a Public Safety Officer seriously affected his bearing. The county police had merely taken a statement from Jamal regarding what he witnessed upon his arrival at the scene. Jamal, after an investigation of his own, came to learn that the story was a bit more complicated.

The timing was shortly after the Charlottesville incident in August of 2017. That Fall the college football team had an Iranian kicker, Tariq Rahimi, a great soccer player who came to the United States and found himself kicking footballs through a goalpost. He told Jamal that after practice one Thursday, he had been walking through the parking lot on the way to his car when three young men approached him and started spewing white racist comments. Although he was on the football team, Tariq was not very big and found himself frightened and intimidated. They pushed him up against his car. They told him, "Go back where you came from. If we see you again you will regret it." One of the boys pulled a knife, pushed Tariq's head back against the roof of the car exposing his throat and said, "I'll slit your throat the next time I see you." They pushed him to the ground and kicked him a few times. Not hard enough to break anything but plenty hard enough to bruise. Then they walked away.

Tariq did not report the incident. He felt like an outsider and feared the outcome of accusing anyone, without witnesses. According to team members, after Tariq had missed two out of three field goals in the Friday night game, they asked him why he seemed so out of it. He said it was nothing, just had a bad night, but several teammates said they had noticed he was holding his side after the second miss. They pressured him into disclosing what happened the night before. Tariq had several good friends on the team. They were angry and wouldn't let go of trying to identify the guys. They told Jamal that they had scoured the campus on Monday morning and again after practicing that evening. Luke Wilson, a tall skinny blonde wide receiver, Stan Howard and Wil Jones, a tackle and a linebacker walked the campus with Tariq. They said they were on a hunt trying to pick out any one of these three guys. They failed. By mid-week, Tariq had not seen them anywhere and told Wil Jones that he would like to just "let it go."

Jamal then determined what had happened in the minutes before he arrived on the scene. It was late on the next Thursday when Tariq and his three friends exited the locker room after practice. They had each stayed for various reasons. Stan and Wil for the whirlpool, Luke was stretching and going over his receiving routes. Tariq was studying and just hanging out. Likely not wanting to venture out to his car alone. Since the beating a week ago the four of them spent a lot of time together. They told Jamal that Tariq was truly petrified of running into these guys on his own again.

Tariq later told Jamal how it unfolded. "The four of us, Stan, Wil, Luke, and me, had just turned the corner from the back hall where the locker rooms were located. We were heading toward the front doors in the main area where the ticket booth, bulletin boards, and trophy cases are. Two young men with shaved heads and tattoos across their neck had their backs turned to them. They were tacking posters to the bulletin board. As we got nearer, I could see the posters were white supremacy propaganda. The keywords, Identity, American, Front, and Movement, sending a clear message. Stan had called out "Hey, take those down. "One of the men glanced over his shoulder and gave them the finger. "It's a free country. Remember?" They had barely looked back to see who they were talking to.

When we came up behind them, Luke, whose arms were longer than a telephone pole, reached over their heads and yanked down one of the posters. The two of them turned in unison. One wore a cutoff sweatshirt with an American Flag on the front. He was well-muscled and well tattooed. The other was less buffed out, wiry, in workman's clothing, and gave off the tension of a coiled snake. That was how I thought of him, Snake. I was unsure if they recognized me, but I surely recognized them as two of the guys who had beat on me. I nudged Stan and when he looked down at me. I mouthed to him, "it's them." Things went bad when Snake turned to me and hissed, "So raghead, you brought your niggers and a scarecrow for protection? Bullshit idea."

Tariq continued the story. "Wil was on him like a cat. He pushed him to the wall and had his forearm across his throat. They were eyeball to eyeball. Wil seemed unsure as to how far he wanted to take it. Snake looked unfazed. Stan and Luke stepped between them and his friend in the flag sweatshirt, creating a standoff of sorts. I took a few steps back." Tariq went on. "Suddenly I was swept up, a gloved hand over my mouth and the arm of a bear around my midriff. I was pulled off my feet. I looked over my shoulder to see who had hold of me. He was big and seemed to be carrying me away toward the front door. Of course, it was the third guy who had attacked me. I realized we had not noticed him in the glassed-in vestibule at the front entrance. No doubt he was the lookout for his friends and their propaganda posters. The last thing I saw as we backed into the exit was a girl, coming from the Women's Locker Room, seeing what was transpiring, picking up the security phone."

It all sounded crazy to Jamal. Dispatch had said nothing more than "Assault in Progress, Athletic Center."

What Tariq said next was a bit of a jumble. "The big guy who grabbed me didn't speak. He still had his hand over my mouth. My objections and screams for help were completely muffled. I remember being outside and up against the side of the building in the shadows. I saw Luke and Stan push the flag shirted guy out the door and then Wil, with Snake in an armlock, pushing him out right behind them. I heard Luke callout "Tariq?" Before I could even grunt a reply, the guy who had hold of me ran right at everyone and literally threw me into the group, knocking all but himself to the ground. He came at us kicking as his friends jumped up and regained the advantage. It was a brawl. Stan and I had tackled the big guy, Wil dragged Snake to the ground, but Luke was having some trouble with the guy in the flag sweatshirt. In a minute or so, it seemed the well-conditioned athletes had begun to outlast the energy of the others and took control. The last thing I remember was a flash of a metal blade as Snake brought his hand out of his pocket and flicked his wrist. Right then the big guy's elbow connected with my chin and it all went dark. The next thing I remember you were helping me to my feet."

Jamal was indeed the first on the scene. He had to break up the brawl which wasn't really a brawl by then. It had turned into a beating and nearly a death. His statement to the police, and the only part of this he could testify to, began at that moment of arrival. Two African-Americans and a tall Caucasian were standing, bloody and breathless, a big heavily muscled guy was out cold, his face well battered, a tattooed shirtless guy was on one knee, holding a balled-up sweatshirt against the side of a wiry guy on the ground with what appeared to be a knife in his side. Also, on the ground, a few feet away was a middle eastern kid wallowing in dreamland. Jamal recognized the football players from watching practices during his patrol and then realized the other one as the team's Iranian placekicker. Seconds later he had dispatch on the line, requesting an ambulance, and county police.

Jamal unstrapped his holster and drew his gun as trained. He did not feel threatened. Yet training kicked in. In the presence of a knife or any weapon, assume nothing. He announced, "Everyone face down on the ground and spread your arms. Keep your hands where I can see them." They seemed as if the fight was out of them anyway. He checked the wounded guy on the ground. It seemed the other guy knew what he was doing in the first aid department and had staunched much of the blood flow. Jamal said, "keep up what you are doing, ambulance on the way. And don't touch the knife or try to get up. Don't make me shoot you."

The smaller of the players spoke first. "I'm Wil Jones, he said. I did not stab that guy. He came at me with the knife. I grabbed his wrist. He tried to trip me. I spun out and flipped him over my knee. Might have lost my balance then and fell on him. I just heard a grunt and he ceased resisting. I got up and he had the knife in his side."

Jamal thought back to his days as an MP in Iraq. He saw a few of these brawls in his day, but the participants were usually drunk and the beatings less enthusiastic.

The tall lanky player spoke up next. "Officer, these guys beat up our kicker last week and we came out of practice tonight to find them putting up supremacy posters in the gym. Then they grabbed Tariq again and we got into it."

The shirtless guy looked up and snarled, "Liar. You started the fight inside. We were within our rights to hang the posters."

Jamal needed to ratchet this down until the county police showed up. He had to maintain control and certainly did not have handcuffs for everyone. Luckily, the biggest bear of a guy was still asleep. Tariq was starting to stir. By then Jamal could see the flashing lights racing across campus toward the Athletic Center parking lot. Two cruisers pulled up first and four officers spilled out and ran toward the grassy area in front of the entrance. The EMS crew had a stretcher and were quick to load the stabbing victim on it. Now there were handcuffs for all, without regard to who attacked whom, all five participants had questions to answer before they would be set free. Even Tariq, who was clearly still a bit out of it and the big guy whom an officer had rolled over, cuffed him and then it took two of them to drag him to his feet. Jamal finished telling the officers what he knew as two more cruisers pulled up to assist in the transport of the five men to the jail. Jamal was told that the sixth man, a Willis Grant, would be okay once they put some blood back into him and got him stitched up. A few inches either way and he might have bled out.

Jamal felt his official statement would do little to tell the whole story and certainly would not exonerate the players. He felt good about having gone after more of the facts. At least he knew Tariq's side of the story. He was not about to find out more from the skinheads or whatever they were. He had neither the jurisdiction nor the inclination. When the story came out, Jamal felt conflicted about his own feelings. About whether a beating is ever justified. He wished that he had had the good fortune of coming upon those boys the week before and been able to stop them from beating up Tariq in the first place. Not having to be the one who came to the scene and could only offer testimony that might get these students jail time. As a black man, white racism was hard to deal with, but as a policeman, trained in the army, among people from all over the world, he needed to be a professional and he had to enforce the law. There would be nothing Jamal could say in court that would make the boys' actions defensible. He hoped the system would sort it out. Hoped that somewhere in what the boys had told him there was some truth.

Jamal was thinking a bit about the courses he had put off until next year. Sociology, Psychology, and Philosophy. Subjects he had avoided. His background as an abandoned child was a sociological nightmare, would have left many psychologically damaged and left little room for philosophy. After his experience as a Public Safety Officer, he decided those courses would surely be in his sophomore curriculum because they would not be a study about him and his damaged childhood. He would be educated regarding the human condition and help him see the world as it really is.

https://www.insidehigh-
ered.com/news/2019/06/27/white-nationalist-
propaganda-rise-college-campuses

Mom's

For over forty years, nearly every workday I have walked through a door into an office. On that door has been the inscription, Joseph Amato, Attorney-at-Law. My first experience in a law office was in the fall of 1968. My name was not on the door. It was barely on a paycheck. The first sixteen hours a week that I worked was considered an internship for which I was getting two credits at NYU. I did get paid if I worked extra hours, which I did on a regular basis. I loved the buzz. I loved the intensity with which the young lawyers attacked their jobs. It was competitive and cutthroat. I had done two years at Fairleigh Dickenson. Having screwed around in high school, my grades were not going to get me accepted anywhere great, so I stayed home in Fair Lawn and commuted to Teaneck. The deal was, if I could get good grades there in my first two years I could transfer into the city and live in Manhattan. NYU was much more challenging.

Being at the law firm made it worth it. It felt safe. College campuses were in turmoil over the Vietnam War. I was against the war and would have gone to some length to not go. Being out in the streets protesting was not my thing. I also knew that law school would earn me a draft deferment for a while. I graduated from NYU. My grades were good but not great. My advisor counseled me that for a law school, NYU or Columbia were going to be a reach. Money was also an issue. My parents paid for undergraduate school and covered living expenses. I paid my rent in a shared apartment with my law firm paycheck. As for law school, they offered to pay half the tuition and said I could move home until I could afford my own place again.

That's what I did. I got a decent legal education at Seton Hall. I became a partner at the first New Jersey firm I worked for. Married late, mid-thirties, divorced over a dozen years ago. I have a kid who is over thirty now and living in the family home since my ex-wife died. Weird having my son, Neal, living in the house I grew up in. I should visit more. I gave him a raw deal. I was selfish and miserable. I had to leave his mother. I waited until he could go off to college and leave her too. I never thought he would stay around and get caught up in her angst. I've been in California since 2006. I joined a practice here. I went out on my own a few years later. I had passed on coming to California in the 1970s when I did not want to leave my aging parents alone in Fair Lawn. I had come to L.A. for an entertainment law conference and got the bug. But, shortly thereafter, marriage and family living got in the way. Once I walked out of my New Jersey life all those years later, southern California was my destination.

I've lived a good life. At the end of the day, I'm still that teenager, Joey Amato. When I turned seventy years old, I became more reflective. Fair Lawn in the 1950s and 1960s was a small New Jersey town, just eight miles from the George Washington Bridge and New York City. I guess you would consider us suburban kids. People I've known over the years say they should never have survived high school. For Fair Lawn kids who discovered Mombasha's Inn, it was especially true. I'm not about to say that I grew up in an inner-city environment and might have been shot or killed because of rampant street violence. I did, however, grow up in a town that was a bit different from the way many kids grew up in suburbia.

I stopped telling this story because unless there was someone from my high school in the room, no one ever believed me. But it's a fact. It was true that for nearly ten years, kids my high school had an arrangement with a bar in upstate New York. It was nearly an hour away and for the most part only Fair Lawn High School kids would hang out there. The destination had compound risks. It was on a mountain top. The road up was treacherous. Down, after a night at of drinking, deadly.

May 1966

I was in the backseat of Don Field's car. I was seventeen. There were six of us crowded in. Easier back then. Bench seats front and back in the 1960 Plymouth, he had. We were driving north on Route 17. We had passed the state line about a mile back when the flashing lights came up behind us. Not good. We had stopped in Suffern and picked up a sack of Colt 45 forties, luckily had them stashed in the trunk as a backup for later. Much better to be stopped on the way up, sober, then later, on the way home.

Don said, "What the fuck. What shit did I do to get pulled over?" Billy Wells, who was riding shotgun, answered with a question. "Do you think he'll ask where we are going or search the car.?" I thought fast and said,

"Tell the cop we went to a camp up near Monroe, (he and I did) and we are meeting some friends at the Red Apple Rest. Make it sound like it's normal, innocent like we've done it before.

The cop was a state trooper name of Cooper, according to the badge. He ran his flashlight over each of us. Smirking, he said, "Do you know you changed lanes back there without signaling?"

I thought Don would start laughing at the "Trooper Cooper" badge, but he choked out, "No officer, I thought I had. Must not have hit the lever hard enough." I figured the cop was just hassling us. He walked back to his car with Don's license and registration. Spent nearly five minutes "calling it in." When he finally walked back to Don's open driver side window, he handed Don his papers. He again put his flashlight on each of our faces. "What are six Jersey boys doing on a Friday night heading into my fair state? Hmm. What do we have here that New Jersey doesn't? Let me think? I wonder if I asked each of you for id, you'd all be eighteen." Before he could continue Don said, "Yes Officer Cooper, we are eighteen. Three of us worked at Camp Lenape last summer and made some friends up here. Girls. We are meeting them up at the Red Apple Rest then they are taking us to a party. Are you giving me a ticket? We are running a bit late now and don't want the girls to worry."

Don was a great bullshitter, and this was him at his best. I said act normal and he goes for indifferent and arrogant. We in the backseat had slouched down and were barely able to contain hysterics. For a brief instant, I thought the cop was going to laugh too. "No, he said. Just a warning. A car full of teenagers is an accident about to happen. Be careful. Pay attention. Don't give me a reason to stop you again tonight. You can go."

We normally would have bypassed the turn off the road into the Red Apple Rest parking lot and continued another five hundred yards to a slightly hidden left turn that would take us up the mountain toward Momba-sha's. But after the Trooper Cooper incident, we couldn't shake the feeling he was lurking behind us and might come up and check the parking lot for our car. We pulled in and parked. Who said we couldn't eat before we drink? We heard they had good pie.

There had been a buzz around school that afternoon about going up to Mom's tonight. It was a Friday and a good crowd was expected. We rarely ever stopped at the Rest, or anywhere on the road for that matter. We would drive up and back as if it was just a few blocks not, inter-state travel. The Red Apple was an icon on this highway. Two of us had hot dogs, I had a sausage, and the rest had pie. We ate, waited twenty minutes, then set out again. Don had driven up this road quite a few times but rarely was sober enough to drive down. That often fell on me. I didn't drink as much as everyone else. Or at least, I didn't get as drunk. Hard to imagine so many people from one small town in New Jersey would leave the state to go thirty miles north to a mountaintop party at a bar held open to high school students. The drinking age in New Jersey was twenty-one. The drinking age in New York was eighteen. Draft cards did not have pictures and neither did driver licenses. Therefore, no real photo ID was expected in 1966. Eye color, hair color, height and weight. Those were the attributes one was identified by. Fake draft cards were prevalent. Everybody was '*eighteen.*' Well almost everybody. The girls had no draft cards, so they needed fake licenses. I never knew where they came from, but lots of the girls had them. If they didn't, they would sit outside on Mom's porch, and let the guys buy them drinks and bring them out. Nobody seemed to care.

As we progressed up the mountain the boys in the car got quiet. Eager to be there, pondering their interaction with the cop, wondering how they had gotten away from further problems such as their parents being called. I was feeling lucky until Billy screamed," lookout, lookout." We had come to the hairpin turn and for a moment it seemed Don had spaced on it. A quick way to die. The right front tire was spewing gravel as we briefly left the road, but Don slowed, got us under control and laughed out, "What's the problem? Not even close." Ricky Thomas who was in the back seat with me, jammed in the middle straddling the transmission hump, looked a bit green. Finally, the lights of Mombasha's Inn appeared through the trees. We pulled through the back of the already full parking lot and parked in the overflow field behind. There were already more than fifty cars. Coming in groups and doing the math there would likely be over two hundred kids from our high school there tonight.

We could've gone into New York City. It was closer. Twenty minutes over the George Washington Bridge and we were in the Bronx, then another ten minutes we would be in uptown Manhattan, focusing on the area around Columbia University which was ripe with bars. The drawback to the city was that many of us were still seventeen and our fake draft cards did not help the fact that you had to be eighteen to drive in Manhattan. That occasionally gave us pause but was often ignored if Mom's seemed too far because of timing or bad weather. We were also in proximity to Rockland County, New York. Nanuet, Rye, and Portchester had some great bars. Not to forget about Greenwood Lake which sits on the New York/New Jersey border. On the New York side of the lake, bars were readily available to eighteen-year-olds and those of us pretending to be.

The six of us walked through the front door of the bar after briefly hanging out on the porch where there were a couple of large tables. More girls than guys out there. Everyone had a drink in front of them. Once inside we split up. Don and I went to the bar grabbed two stools as they were vacated. Sam, the white-haired bartender who we thought might be the owner, came over. We both ordered screwdrivers. The best dollar drink ever. House vodka and some canned orange juice. Didn't taste great but the vodka went down easy that way.

"Don," I said, "what are we doing up here again tonight?" Don replied, "What do you mean? Where else would we be? All our friends are here." In a lyrical voice, he sang, "I'm in with the in-crowd, I go where the in-crowd goes."

I smiled, "Yeah, right. The in-crowd, but still alone. Julie and I are done. You and Karen are done. We're here thinking that the girls we see every day in the hall will suddenly be all into us. Dream on."

Don retorted, "This bar may be filled with girls from our high school, but some magical transition occurs when they reach Moms. No longer are they, uptight teenagers, spinning the combination to their locker and looking away if you glance at them. These are girls with a buzz.

They have a need. I have a need. It's about tonight. Not tomorrow."

"Dream on young Spartan," I quipped. Then I threw down the rest of my drink. Down the bar I caught sight of Billy Wells, tossing back beer after beer. Giggling and laughing with two girls who were not that familiar. Although our football players discouraged guys from other towns from coming here, girls were always welcome. A blonde in our class named Peggy reached between Don and me, trying to flag the bartender. I got up, offered her my seat. She said, "thanks, Joey. You are always so sweet." Don spun his stool so to be facing Peggy. "Hi Peg. Screwdriver? He had ordered two more for us, and Sam, the bartender was just placing one in front of Don, and then hesitated, not sure, but put the other down in front of Peggy. He gave me an apologetic look. As I walked away Don had his arm on her shoulder and I heard her ask, "Is it true you and Karen are over?" "For good this time, he said. By the time I got to the other end of the bar, they were laughing and hugging. Maybe it would be Don's night after all.

"Hey Joey," Billy said, "what's shaking? That was quite a ride up tonight, wasn't it? So glad we made it, he slurred. "You may want to slow down on the beer, Billy, I replied, we still need to get home in one piece." "I'm good, choir boy. Why don't you loosen up? I'm going outside to see what I can see. Catch you later, Saint Joey.

I ordered a beer and carried it out to the porch. A perky cheerleader named Barbara was holding court at one of the larger round tables. We were old friends. Never dated. The table was a mix of friends and acquaintances. I took the empty seat next to Barbara. She turned toward me first, then she scanned her audience. Appearing semi-lucid but dreamy she said, "I wonder where our parents think we are. We trained them by staying out until one or two in the morning ever since we started high school. True, we were around town, on foot, safe in our little suburban enclave. Now they buy it when we say we are hanging out at somebody's house. When our older friends got their driver licenses and we were able to start leaving town. No one was the wiser. Now we sit on this mountaintop, get loaded, and we still wander in sometime between one and two in the morning. My parents are clueless. I assume they all are." Everybody around the table laughed. I said, "I'll drink to that." And drink they did. I went on a drink run into the bar and brought out a tray of whiskey shots. Of course, I only had one. I was Saint Joey after all.

Suddenly, Angela, one of the Pom girls, ran up the back stairs coming up from the lakeside. "Hurry, hurry," she said. "Billy's down by the lake on all fours and I think he's throwing up blood." We all jumped up from the table, leaped down the stairs, and ran down the hill to the lake. Sure enough, Billy was down on his knees. The pool of vomit on the ground in front of him was red. Angela screamed, "Oh my god. We need to get him to a hospital." Don walked out from the trees holding hands with Peggy and sauntered over. He calmly knelt next to Billy patted him on the back. "Are you all right?" Billy just grunted, "I think so." Don took out a Zippo lighter and flipped it to get a flame so he could see what was on the ground. A very red pool of puke stared back at him. And then Don started laughing hysterically. "Hey Joey, what kind of pie did Billy have when we stopped at the Rest?"

I thought for a second and responded with a chuckle, "Cherry, I think." Don looked up at everyone who had gathered. "Well, it's cherry pie on the ground, not blood. Nothing to see here. Go back to drinking." A roar of approval sent the group in various directions. Don and Peggy, back toward the tree line, Billy had rolled away from his deposit of cherry pie and Angela was sitting in the grass beside him, gently stroking his head. The group from our table headed back up the hillside to re-occupy the porch. Barbara reached out for my hand as if she needed some leverage to get back up the hill, but as the slope leveled, she held on, smiled and said, "Would you sit out front on the porch swing with me? I'm a little tired and don't want to drink anymore."

There was very little activity to the left of the front door where the porch swing was dappled with moonlight. The larger porch was around the other side with a view of the lake beyond. The field for parking stretched out into the darkness. Barbara's head was on my shoulder and she was whispering in my ear. "You know I've always liked you, Joey? Remember fifth grade. We sat in the same row. You were behind me and kept kicking my chair. I'd get mad and turn around just like you wanted me to. You'd wink and pucker and make faces, so I'd laugh, just enough so the next thing I'd hear was Mr. Hall; *"Barbara, please turn around and stop fooling around with Joey."* I'd be so mad. But I loved those faces you made."

I never felt that Barbara, or any of the pretty blonde cheerleaders, would ever consider me as a boyfriend. I was dark, Italian looking, not tall enough for basketball, not big nor quick enough to make the football team and

I hated soccer. I wrestled a couple of seasons, was strong for my size but could never beat the starter in my weight class, thus I was relegated to junior varsity. Completely on the fringe of any in-crowd.

The alcohol must have loosened my tongue, as I heard myself stupidly say, "I never felt good enough for you." Barbara bolted upright. "Joey Amato, you are an idiot. You are going to do great things in your life. Everyone you know likes you. Some might even love you. You need to be in the moment and feel more. You tend to hold back a lot. If you were paying attention you would have noticed that you always make me laugh. Great relationships have been based on a lot less."

I had heard enough. My arms went around her, and my alcohol loosened tongue was suddenly halfway down her throat. Barbara was making sounds that seemed to have been pent up since fifth grade. My heart and my jeans were both about to explode when over my shoulder I heard—.

"Oh my god, Joey. I've been looking all over for you."

It was Karen, Don's ex. She was sloshed. "Julie needs you. We came up in her car, Kathy, Val and me. We are all so wasted. But Julie, she's done for. Plastered. She passed out on the way to the parking lot. Kathy threw water on her and she woke up and mumbled, "*Find Joey, he will be sober as a judge. Get him to take us home.*" Then she threw up and passed out again, Karen said."

I stood up and gave Barbara a shield so she could gather herself. I was not happy. Julie knew we were done. Drunk or not she has no right to do this to me. She knows I'll do it. Not let her down. Even if her standard practice was to cheat on me then lie about it.

I said, "Okay, you are all too drunk to drive. Do you have Julie's keys?" Barbara stood up beside me. She gave me the stink eye look and said, "*I thought you were free of Julie.*" I kissed her on the cheek and whispered, "Sorry, I've got to do this. Do me a favor and tell Don I left so he won't look for me. I'll make it up to you, I promise. Do you have a ride home?" She nodded and turned away without another word.

By the time we got back to Fair Lawn, all four girls were fast asleep. Kathy, Karen and I could all walk home from Julie's house. I needed to wake Val first and drop her at her house. Karen was in the front with me, so I reached over and shook her awake. "Hey Karen, roust your minions, we are back and need to get everyone home."

When we pulled up in front of Val's house, Kathy got out with her and got her halfway up the walk before Val waved her off and claimed to be fine. When Kathy got back in the car, I told them the plan. I would park Julie's car in front of her house and disappear. I certainly did not want to see her parents who were still not happy we'd broken up in the first place. They felt I was a good influence on their daughter. No argument from me that Julie needed some good influences to offset her less than truthful nature.

I doused the headlights two houses up from Julie's and coasted silently to a stop. I reached up and flicked the overhead light off so we could open the doors without attracting attention from inside the house. Julie was still doing the sleep of the dead. She was not very big and alcohol consumption was not her strong suit. I put her over my shoulder, Kathy grabbed Julie's handbag, Karen locked the car and tossed Kathy the keys to put in Julie's bag. When we stepped up onto the porch, Julie was stirring. I put her down on the front doormat. Karen turned her sideways and sat her up, placing Julie's right hand on the door handle. Karen waved us off the porch, rang the doorbell and ran. We followed her around the side of the house into the darkness.

Fun to browse:

https://www.messynessychic.com/2017/04/27/if-only-the-decaying-walls-of-the-iconic-red-apple-rest-stop-could-talk/

Author's note: "Mom's" is based on actual events that took place in Fair Lawn, New Jersey, and Upstate New York in the 1960s. Of course, it is the least believable of the collection.

As a thank you to those who offered up fuel for the story, I include quotes offered by some classmates:

"Mombasha's in Orange County NY was the destination to get sloshed, loaded, tanked up, or plain drunk. Guys used to brag that they miraculously drove home arriving in one piece."

"In Fair Lawn, N.J. in the mid-1960's Mombasha's was a rite of passage. It wasn't available to all. It was only available when an upperclassman would reach out and invite you to go. I didn't know where or what it was about…but the unknown was calling. Somehow, we knew it was fun, dangerous, and important."

"I remember having a drinking contest with Flo at the bar. The bartender handed me another drink and said this is from the guy down at the end of the bar. It was my brother glaring at me! He was so mad at me for being there! LOL Yeah, good times! Ha-ha"

"I have a vague recollection of the porch and it being back in the woods. Remote. Moms had a bad boy vibe and allure that made you want to experience it."

"As many times as I went to Mombasha's, I couldn't tell you how I got there or where it really was. The darkness was a factor. And I never did the driving. So, it all remains a blur. A blur of excitement and danger. My last night at Mom's kind of says it all. It was either the night of graduation in June of 1966 or a day or two before. The rite of passage that Mom's represented to us was about to become another symbol of passage…from high school to college and beyond."

EPILOGUE - NEXT
MOTHER'S DAY

Fort Lee, New Jersey

Neal was awakened by the sound of an incoming text message. He reached for his phone on the nightstand. He saw the time was 9:06 and he had slept in. He had closed the restaurant last night and gotten home late. He could sleep in because he was not going to work today. It was Friday. He had worked late all week in order to get a schedule where he could be off all weekend. The benefit of being a manager. Sunday was Mother's Day. He was going to make it memorable.

The text was from his realtor. It simply said, *"Call me. I have an offer on the house."* Mixed feelings? Right in his gut. Selling the house in Fair Lawn. The house his father grew up in. The house his mom had died in, then left to him. The house he also grew up in and where he went into hiding after Mom died. Yeah, that house. It was time. He had moved out last fall and begun freshening it up to put on the market. Neal even hired a staging outfit to make it look a bit less like last century. By September he had stopped sleeping there at all. He was spending every night in Fort Lee. Liz did not like extending her commute by sleeping over in Fair Lawn. She had been a big help with the final cleanout and preparation for sale. They agreed that he would get a storage unit for his "stuff." Her apartment had room for him, but not everything he owned. She had kissed him and said, "You can bring it all out again when we get our house."

Things had happened fast once they found out how much they liked spending time together. Last Mother's Day he hit bottom. Liz brought him back. They liked the same music. Her brother had been a big influence on her taste. Neal knew they were attracted to each other on that first night. Once they got past the age thing. Neal made the case that if he was turning forty and she was thirty-two it would seem perfectly normal to fall in love, get married and have a family. Making a big deal about it was ageism and surely some kind of gender bias issue. And to boot, her clock was ticking. Loud. At the end of the day, she wanted to be a mother.

Neal had not felt this good about anything or anyone in his entire life. So, there it was. It started with a few more dinners. Then breakfast on Sunday. Then concerts in the city. The Bowery Ballroom, The Rockwood Music Hall. Jazz in the Village. Then he began sleeping over. Good thing he had held off getting a dog. He envisioned a new house, their house, a fenced yard for a dog, and a swing set for the child. And clearly, as of this morning, not the house in Fair Lawn where the past resided. Good memories and bad. The past, not the future.

Back in March, when the house was about ready to be listed, Neal called his father. He had not seen him since Mom's funeral. He had spoken to him once, over a year ago. It was during a downtime. Before he met Liz. Back when he was wallowing in self-pity. It is no wonder his dad had not reached out since. Joseph Amato, Santa Monica, California, attorney, had a new life and a new wife. Neal told his dad about the many changes in his life. About Liz, how they met, that they were having a child together, but not married. Mainly, Neal asked for his father's blessing on selling what was originally his family home beginning in 1954. His dad's response was positive. He said he had waited a long time for his son to find his place in the world and someone to share it with. He never thought that place was going to be in an old house off River Road in Fair Lawn. Dad admitted major guilt over leaving the instant Neal had turned eighteen. In hindsight, realizing that Neal was then left to deal with the woman he could no longer live with. The result of reconnecting with his father was a plan for him and Liz, still just in her second trimester, to fly out to L.A. for Father's Day.

More imminent was Mother's Day weekend. To-night, he and Liz were going to Newark Airport to pick up the Tanners. Liz's mom and dad were coming to spend the holiday weekend in New York City and meet the "*boy*" their daughter had "*taken up with.*" He had been hoping that her brother Mark and his family would also come to provide a buffer. He and Liz had flown out to Austin at Christmas for a few days. Neal was sure that the reason he and Liz were still together was that he had gotten Mark's "*seal of approval.*" Liz had not told her mom about the trip. She hated keeping secrets, but Liz knew a loaded gun when she saw one. After all, she had grown up in Texas.

Neal escaped his reverie long enough to open the favorites on his phone and hit the "Liz" button. It was right on top, above the fateful "Mom" button. It rang twice and she answered and said, "Good morning sleepy head. You never even stirred when I got up, showered, dressed, and intentionally made noise. I wanted a kiss goodbye."

"Sorry babe, he said excitedly, we have an offer on the house. If it goes through, we can start house hunting and maybe find a place before the baby comes."

Liz laughed, "It seems we are on a freight train gathering speed young squire. But, yes Neal, I'd like that. In the meantime, we need to deal with Mother's Day and the woman who you might just need to call "Mom" someday."

"Is that a proposal, Ms. Tanner? Whatever I call her, it will still be Mrs. Tanner in my contacts. *Mom* is still reserved. But I do promise, no texting."

Columbia, Maryland

Forty-eight hours later and just over two hundred miles south, a text came into a phone that was sitting on a kitchen counter. It both buzzed and vibrated. Alice Miller had her hands on a ball of cookie dough she was about to roll out and cut into fun-shaped sugar cookies. She leaned over to read the message." *Happy Mother's Day, Mom.*" Of course, it had come from her seemingly adopted son, Jamal Miller as he was now known. What a change from her life on Mother's Day morning a year ago. She had literally been the one who was adopted. Adopted and taken in by Jamal and Kim and their entire extended family. Playing the role of mother to Jamal, grandmother to the growing baby girl, while trying to avoid having the Li family see her as an intruding in-law.

And then there are the Bloom's. Mike and Maggie have been so sweet. They had also become good friends over the course of the year. After a contrite Mike Bloom showed up at her door on the Monday evening after last Mother's Day with two dozen roses and tears in his eyes. He had gotten her name from the policeman while signing the accident report. He called the next morning and apologized for his recklessness and said he needed to hear her say she was alright. She told him a bit about her own distraction. What had led to her not paying attention to her surroundings. Mike had also become friends with Jamal. He had checked with the hospital Sunday evening and was told Alice Miller had been released. That prompted the follow-up call to Alice on Monday. When she told him the story, he insisted on meeting Jamal. He told Jamal about his Mother's Day weekend leading up the accident and turned him on to Charm City Helicopter Tours. Now Jamal was flying co-pilot on weekends to make extra money.

Today, on the anniversary of the accident, she was being picked up early by the Bloom family, to go for coffee by the lake. Then they were going to drop her at the Li's for the Mother's Day festivities before they drove down to Silver Spring to do the same with Mike's mom. If she hurried, she would be able to get the cookies out of the oven and cooled enough to pack a box for Jake and Annie Bloom and another box for Jamal's family.

Once the cookies were in the oven and she had washed and dried her hands, she picked up her phone and opened it to the text message screen. She quickly typed a text to Mike. *"On schedule. You can pick me up at 10:30."* Then she scrolled to the previous message.

The one from Jamal. She didn't write anything. Instead, she sent three heart emojis. She had this cell phone thing down. After all, where would she be today without it?

AFTERWORD

Thank you for reading my first collection of stories. Mother's Day was at the heart of the stories and the "other stories," all relate to the characters introduced in those first two stories. It may even seem a novella.

I want to be clear. These stories are pure fiction except for the premise of Mom's story as noted at the story's end. There was a Mombasha's Inn and I presented events as they may have happened, with loads of fictional latitude.

Instances where real places or events are mentioned in a story, I have the most interesting web links at the end of the story. I may have made up the stories, but I love to share the real locations where they were said to take place. Have fun browsing.

I have done many other things in my life. Writing stories and actually finishing them is a bit new. I hope over time I become a better writer. For now, these stories were swirling around in my head and wanted to be told. I hope you've enjoyed reading them.

Social Media being what it is, I look forward to hearing from readers on varied platforms.

For Email: Info@RoamingtheArts.com

Visit **RoamingtheArts.com** to explore a dynamic re-source for those interested in music, books, and art.

ACKNOWLEDGMENTS

Thank you to my editor, Dan Barden, and my primary beta readers, Stephanie Kelly, Amy Witzke, and, Linda Leibowitz Rosen, all of whom made numerous suggestions and edits, hopefully resulting in much-improved stories. Any errors which remain are entirely on me.

Thank you, Michael Oberman, for allowing me to use one of your fabulous photographs for the cover. The field of Tulips representing spring and offering a colorful Mother's Day feeling was taken in Columbia, Maryland. So fitting.

Thank you, Joe Kelly, for allowing me to borrow your name for the policeman. Thank you, Roger Blevins Jr., for telling me the story about the band. Thank you to the Mansion on O St. for being a treasure in Washington D.C. Many thanks to all the friends and family who have made cameo appearances by name and pseudonym. Thank you for being in my life.

There are many other people to thank. I had often asked friends to listen to these storylines over the last two years. Thank you all for being so patient.